T0090294

Dragon Born

Christopher Lee

Order this book online at www.trafford.com
or email orders@trafford.com

Most Trafford titles are also available at major online book retailers.

Printed in the United States of America.

ISBN: 978-1-4269-3641-8 (soft)
ISBN: 978-1-4269-3642-5 (hard)
ISBN: 978-1-4269-3752-1 (ebook)

Library of Congress Control Number: 2010909200

*Our mission is to efficiently provide the world's finest, most comprehensive book publishing
service, enabling every author to experience success. To find out how to publish your
book, your way, and have it available worldwide, visit us online at www.trafford.com*

Trafford rev. 7/14/2010

 www.trafford.com

North America & international
toll-free: 1 888 232 4444 (USA & Canada)
phone: 250 383 6864 ♦ fax: 812 355 4082

Thanks for all of the help to Harkerit Takher

If you only look at your failures,
how do you expect to see your successes.

Chapter One

Tamara was really pissed, she had rented a car for this very reason. Now here she was walking in the night, down this dark country road like something out of a horror story and according to the last sign she was eight miles from the nearest town, all because her rented car had broken down. She calculated the distance in her head, at four miles per hour walking speed, that was two hours. If she jogged from time to time that might cut the time by half an hour. Great she would jog into town at two thirty in the morning. She checked her phone again, still no signal. That was strange, what did the people that lived in this town do without cell phone service? She had just started to jog when she heard a car coming up from behind her. She had already made up her mind not to be seen. She felt safer walking in to town then trusting someone for a ride. She was lucky the moon was full, it lit the way as she moved into the bushes at the side of the road to let the car pass. The road here was cleaved from the side of the mountain leaving a steep drop on one side and a very steep rise on the other. As she hunkered down behind a bush so she wouldn't be seen by the person in the car, and in the quiet she heard a deep rumbling growl off in the distance and down the hillside behind her. She was holding precariously on to a shrub and crouching down, letting the surrounding shrubs shield her from the car's lights as it went by. After the car passed she began to pull herself up by the shrub she had been holding onto when it snapped. Letting out a hyphenated scream she tumbled over backward, crashed through some bushes, careened off a small tree hitting her back against it. Just as she felt herself falling off into open space, the crook of her arm caught on a root sticking up. She grabbed it with her other hand and she dangled there her feet trying to find purchase. She switched so her other hand that was holding the root, she twisted and turned trying to look behind herself to find a way to get down. There was nothing but open air.

Tamara looked for a way to move to her right or her left but all the shrubs and trees were far to small, to hold her weight. Tamara looked down, but all she saw was darkness, she could not tell how far it was below her, but it was to far to let go and fall, she was sure of that. She tried not to panic, she had always been able to keep her cool in a tight, but this had her terrified. She became even more terrified when a large shape passed between her and the moon. She screamed as something gripped her on both shoulders and with a rush of air pulled her away from the ledge, the grip on her shoulders was gentle but firm as she flew upward for a moment, and then downward. After what must have been less then ten seconds, she saw a moonlit grassy area and the downward motion intensified. The air rushed by and she closed her eyes not wanting to look as the ground rushed up. Her feet felt solid ground and she tumbled onto the ground, scratching her elbow on a small stone. She opened her eyes and pushed herself to her feet, turning she found a man who looked to be around twenty five standing there. He had a smirk on his face and not a thread of clothing on, but she could see that he was not self conscious about it at all. His eyes held hers for a small time, Tamara straightened her self up, doing her best to make her voice firm and confident, doing her best to hide the terror that threatened to bring her to her knees.

Who the hell are you? It didn't come out as planned, her voice squeaked as she spoke, her face became red because of it. The man chuckled, I just saved your life and my name is Acacia, as in the tree. I was named that in hopes I would be strong and true. How did you happen to be hanging up there? I fell, she answered, I was hiding behind a bush because a car was coming by, I slipped. How did you get me down? He didn't say anything. She hesitated, this was very weird. She decided to change the subject, do you always go around naked? He didn't even flinch at that. I do sometimes, he answered, when the feeling hits me just right. Why were you hiding from a car? To avoid people like you, she snapped at him. He just shrugged. There was a flapping of wings and a whoosh of air, she screamed and turned to the sound behind her, another man stood there, flawless in his physique as Acacia was. Sorry to startle you, he said in a deep voice, smooth as whipped butter. Another whoosh and a sound to her right, she didn't even flinch. Hello, came a soprano. Acacia walked into her view again, This is William, he motioned to the deep voiced one and Timothy, he motioned to the last one. Tamara looked toward the way his hand motioned. Another naked man, he looked Italian. What the hell is going on! she screamed, naked man convention? Acacia chuckled again, you are among friends I assure you. I told you not to save her, Timothy said, didn't I tell you she would be ungrateful.

A smile touched his eyes and he winked at her. We have a car not far from here, Acacia said, we can take you to your destination. He walked over to a stump that Tamara hadn't noticed, picked up a piece of clothing she recognized as one of those form fitting boxers and slipped them on. Tamara felt herself get wet at the sight, something stirred in her groin area, she blushed again and was thankful it was dark, none of them would have noticed. The others were dressing and Acacia asked her again where she wanted them to take her to. Who are you guys? Acacia, I need to know before I ride anywhere with you. I have a home not to far from here, Acacia said, you can go there if you want an answer. If not, we will drop you off and you can go your way. She looked into his eyes searching. She had an unfounded trust in him He was like a man she had fantasized about often in her life. He was exactly like the man she thought would come and sweep her off her feet. And the trust she felt, trust that she didn't understand. Also, there was something going on here that seemed to verge on supernatural, and she wanted to know what. Again their gaze lingered for a short time into each others eyes. Fine, she told her self, she would go with them to their home, after all she didn't believe in the supernatural. Her thoughts moved toward new technology, they must be testing some new technology, they were doing amazing things with technology. May be enhancement through gene therapy. I want to know more about you guys, I'll go with you to your home, she wanted to get to know this man better. This is going to sound like a cliché, Acacia said, but are you sure you really want to? It will change you forever, Acacia warned her. Will it stop me from getting to my appointments tomorrow? He shook his head, shouldn't. I have a rental car on the road up there some where, would you help me with it later? She asked. Sure, he said, we'll get on it in the morning.

They had been walking together, following the other two, they walked up a slight incline, Acacia swept a limb out of their way that she hadn't been able to see. A few minuets later he led her around a large rock, she hadn't seen either. She looked at him as they walked, how had he seen the limb and the rock when she hadn't, it must be gene therapy she concluded. They walked out into a clearing, the car is here he said, gesturing with his hand. He led her toward a limo parked in a small area beside the road. There were six doors in the side of the limo, he opened a rear door for her and went around to the other side. She slipped into the luxurious black leather seat as he slid in beside her, that was when she noticed his eyes. They were a deep color, but she couldn't tell what color, they seemed to shift colors in the limo's lamp. The other two slipped into a seat in front of them. Tamara made out a driver as he switched on the engine and the lights came on. You seem to have gotten over your fright, you need a drink or anything? You have a water? She asked. To answer her, he opened a small refrigerator door to the left of them. She took the water from his proffered hand, as she did his hand brushed hers and she shivered as an electric tingle moved up her spine. You cold he asked? No, she answered, no, not in this weather. Where do you live, he asked. You said a rental car, you live far? Arizona, close to the middle, she said purposely being vague in her description. That's not to far, had you just started your trip? Yea, headed for New Mexico. My place is about ten minuets ahead, he said, we'll be there shortly. She decided to try finding out about him again. You are a real mystery, do you work for the government? No, I have a business of my own. Profitable I would say, judging from the limo and driver. Some what, he agreed. Here it is, he said, they turned down a lane, and in the limo's light she caught a glimpse of a large modern estate through a break in the trees. They rounded a turn in the lane and drove up in front of a beautiful well lit mansion.

This is beautiful, she said admiringly as she exited the limo. An elderly man open the large front doors as they approached. Welcome home sir, he said, nodding toward Acacia. Thanks Brent. Brent could you prepare a small meal and drinks and serve them in the library. Certainly sir, he answered turning and walked out of the room. Acacia led Tamara, hooking his arm in hers. You can clean up in there, he said, motioning to a door. I'm going in there to freshen up, he said, motioning toward another door, if you need anything I'll be in there, he pointed again toward the door, then I'll wait for you back here, he pointed to where they were standing. The light caught his eyes again, they looked scarlet colored but she couldn't see for sure. You will find almost anything you need, he added, so feel free. Thanks, she said, as she walked through the door and closed it. Inside she found a opulent bath, and a large walk in closet. She leaned against the wall for a moment to think, she didn't feel threatened, actually the opposite, she felt safe. She inspected the closet and found various items she could wear. She saw the shower in the corner and decided to have a quick shower. So she slipped out of her clothes, and into a huge shower, quickly showered and headed for the closet. She found a gorgeous evening gown, looked it over tempted, then placed it back. Came across a nice top and some jeans and chose them. She also found some under clothes with the tags on them and was dressed in no time. True to his word he was standing, waiting for her outside of the door. He took her hand, the same tingle ran up her spine, it felt good and a little foreboding at the same time, she shivered again. The others are waiting in the library for us, shall we go? Yes, she said breathlessly as he proffered his arm.

William and Timothy were talking and laughing over drinks when Acacia opened the door to the library and led Tamara in. Ah, there you are, they said to Acacia. They each bowed over Tamara's hand, kissing it in the old fashioned way. Tamara smiled, she loved the way they treated her as a lady. You are looking very nice, William said in that deep smooth voice of his. Thank you, Tamara said. There was a small cart with plates and utensils, and chaffing dishes filled to the brim with meats and salads and some bread. Help yourself, Acacia said to her, motioning toward the cart. Thanks, she answered, and followed Timothy as he moved about the cart placing items onto a plate, Acacia close behind her. They all settled into a setting area. Acacia seated himself by her and spoke as he ate. She noticed that the other two listened intently. First my full name is Acacia Sebastian Romani, I am just short of nine hundred years old and I have an interest in you in the form of a proposition. She started to protest, he shushed her with a finger over her mouth. I will prove it all in good time, he said. William and Timothy were watching her intently. Here touch my skin, he held his hand out to her. She touched it and that tingle went down her spine again. No here rub it. She rubbed the back of his hand, she shivered again with the tingle that ran down and then up her spine. She looked up at him, your skin has a weird texture. She touched his face. It's that way all over? Yes, it's dragon skin when we are in the human form. She laughed at him for a second then stopped, it made sense. Dragon, she said feeling it in her mouth, letting it slide off her tongue? Yes we, he pointed to the other two, we are dragons. I don't believe in dragons, she said. Well not believing in a thing doesn't make it any less true. We are form shifters. It takes a tremendous amount of energy to change, that is why we eat now to replace the energy we used out there to change. That, he went on, is also the reason why we were naked, we would ruin our clothing if we didn't remove them. I took you from the side of the hill in my talons when it looked very likely you were going to fall and hurt yourself. I saved your life, and could, only because I could fly. Give me an hour, and I will have rested it is better, I'll have more strength to change for you. He paused for a moment as if giving something deep thought. He spoke again. There is something else I want from you. What is that? She asked. This is going to sound very strange and there are a lot of details I will have to tell you later, and they will help you make your decision. I do not want you to be put off by my request but the basic thing is this, I would like you to bear my child. What! she jumped up. You are an ass, she exclaimed shaking her finger at him, I don't even know you! I told you to let her fall, Timothy said. Tamara was embarrassed, he had just asked her to have sex with him in front of his friends. You are jerks she said, all of you. You may have saved my life, but that doesn't give you the right to treat me like a cheap whore, to be treated how ever you please, just because I came to your home with you. They were all staring at her. You are right, Acacia said, that was calloused. I'm sorry Tamara, but we are so desperate. Let me explain farther.

We as dragons only mate to bear children every twelve years. My time is almost up this cycle. William and Timothy barely made it in time for this cycle. When I saw you hanging there and knew if I helped you, I would already be exposing my self to you for what I am, I hoped that you might be willing to let me proposition you and that you might consider being a mother to my child. I can see now I was mistaken, his eyes clouded and his head dropped a little. I can make you financially comfortable, but I would prefer not to have you by bribe. I was hoping you would be willing because of love, that if we had time to get to know each other you could come to care about me. You don't have to decide today, we could get to know each other, maybe you could learn to love me, he was pleading. William spoke, You have to do it willingly, knowing what we are and still be willing. You don't know how hard it is, when most women see us in our dragon form they run away, very few say yes. I would love you until the day you die and take care of you, I have the means and the heart for that, Acacia said. Tamara was staring at her hands, I have a question, Tamara said. Ask it, Acacia prompted her. Do you always talk to your girl friends in front of your guy friends like this, because that might be a lot of your problem. They all looked at each other, Acacia spoke, well yes because this concerns all of us and we are comfortable being open about it. You will eventually have to be comfortable about it also, Acacia went on, as there is something else that you have to know before you say yes. We would have gotten to it if you were agreeable with what we have already told you, but here it is a head of time. Acacia took a deep breath, we will be mating in front of the circle, and by circle that is all the dragons of our group. Tamara coved her face with her hands, trying to shut everything else out. After a few moments of her arguing with her self in her mind on how stupid she was and what will these, these what ever they were think of her, she came instantly to a decision.

Ok, she said, then I want to see your other shape to prove you are not just pulling my chain. Tamara was bad about making spur of the moment decisions, she did it often in her opinion, and she was kicking herself even now about it but she couldn't seem to stop. Acacia looked at William, will you check and make sure

Brent is sleeping, William nodded affirmative and left. When he gets back, and if Brent is asleep, we will go outside in the back and I will change to my dragon form for you. After a few minuets William came back and said Brent was sleeping soundly. They all followed Acacia to the patio where he stripped off his clothing and walked out onto the lawn. William leaned over to her and said, this happens fast and no matter how many times I have seen it, it is still amazing. As Tamara without blinking watched, there was a whoosh and a cloud of what looked like smoke moved out from Acacia, after mere seconds it cleared, and a dragon was standing where Acacia had stood, resting on it's haunches. Tamara involuntarily stepped back. That's him? She asked William. Yes. You can go to him and touch him if you like, he wont care. Tamara moved toward the dragon, when she was close enough, she placed her hand on it's side rubbing the blood red scales. The head came around to look at her close, the pupils of the eyes looked as if a coal of fire was deep inside them and they glowed with a mesmerizing light. The ears resembled a cats with tufts of hair at the top. The back legs were large, ending in clawed feet. Smoke from the nostrils of the dragon got into her eyes causing them to water. She moved toward the tail. It was thick at the haunches, and thinned rapidly to a double barbed point. The dragon moved it's tail and brought the point up to tickle her under one arm. She swatted it away giggling. She moved back to the head and noticed Timothy watching her intently. What? she asked him, as she rubbed the side of the head, the scales were small and softer feeling there. I was thinking maybe he was right, Timothy said. Right about what? She asked. About you, he said. He told us you were special. He's beautiful, she said. The dragon gave her a little kiss on the cheek, she slapped him away. She walked up between his front legs, they were more like arms and hands then legs. She looked up at them, she would have to reach up to touch them. She peered down between his back legs. William came up beside her, what are you doing? I'm looking for his thing. What thing? William prompted her. You know, his thing. Oh,

William said, his member. The dragon's head came up beside her opposite of William. William shrugged at the dragon. Tamara turned to the head and whispered, Where is your dick? She asked Acacia. William snickered and pointed to a flap of scales barley noticeable down close to the ground. Tamara looked to where he was pointing, she crouched down and opened the flap, she gasped and backed out to the front of the dragon. I can't, it is to big, that would hurt and might not fit. There was the whoosh of air that she now knew was the sound the dragons made in changing, and a naked Acacia was saying, no you misunderstood. We mate in this form, not the dragon form.

Tamara started laughing, she heard William and Timothy laughing so hard they were gasping for breath. Acacia started laughing as well and after they all had settled down, Tamara went over to Acacia, I'm sorry, she said. No, please don't be sorry, he told her. I guess, she said, I guess I really don't understand what you want from me. Acacia looked at her for a moment. Ok let me start from the beginning, let's go inside and sit down, I'm getting cold out here, I want to dress. Ok, she agreed. As they walked inside she heard William and Timothy snickering. I'm sorry if I embarrassed you in front of your friends, she told Acacia. William answered her, please no, he said, we haven't laughed so hard in so long I can't even remember. Timothy nodded his head in agreement. But I will tell you that if we weren't so desperate, I doubt Acacia would have let anyone open his flaps. He burst into laughter again tears running down his face. Timothy was crying with laughter also, I can't, it's to big, he said between bouts, repeating what she had said when she had opened his flap. Acacia reached over and pushed Timothy in a playful way, enough, he said now let's explain this to her. After he was clothed and settled into a seat he said, here is how it is. First, as a dragon we mate for children once every twelve years. Can you have sex any other time? She asked. We are the same as men otherwise, we can only procreate every twelve years. Why didn't you plan for this ahead of time if you know all of that. Timothy spoke, we did, we had a mate for him but she died. How did she die, Tamara asked, now maybe she would get the truth. She wrecked his Ferrari. His Ferrari? Yea, William said, right up on that road where you say your rental is. Do you have a mate? Tamara asked William. My mate is pregnant with my child, he said. Your going to be a dad? Yes, he said. What about you? She asked Timothy. My mate is with child also. The thing is, Acacia said, their children will die at birth if I don't have a child as well, that's the way it is. The others nodded agreement. Why? she asked, what makes you so special? I'm like a prince, he said, or maybe a leader, as if anyone should understand how that mattered. So, she said, you will have to do better then that.

Well in a circle of dragons, he began to explain, the life of the prince's child insures the life of the other children, it may seem strange to you but that is the way it is. So this is what you are trying to tell me, Tamara asked. You and I make love like normal, with you in this form. She went on, and I get pregnant, then what? You will have a baby boy, and as long as our child is alive the other children will continue to live. Acacia said. A boy, not a girl? She asked. Always, they all said in unison. A human boy? Tamara asked. No, Acacia said a dragon boy, every time. I've never had sex before, does that matter. They all looked at each other. It matters doesn't it, she asked. No they said in unison again. How old are you Tamara? Acacia asked. Nineteen. You are a virgin? Yes, her chin went up, I was saving myself for the man I love. So you will not bear my child? he asked, disappointment thick in his words. Not if you will not marry me first. There was a pause, Dragon's do not marry, Acacia said. They do now, Tamara said. Acacia thought on this a moment. I will live and not age as you get old and die, he said looking her in the eye. I liked you from the time I first saw you, Tamara said, I can live with that. I can not say I love you at this moment, he said. You might later, she answered. You promise to see to my needs for the rest of my life? She asked him. I will take good care of you all of the rest of your life, he swore to her, if you will do this thing for me. I will do it then she said, but we marry tomorrow, no ceremony, just a judge and later if you don't mind we could have a ceremony. Done, he said. She stood up, take me and make love to me then, let's give you a child and save the other children. William sat down, a shocked look on his face. I'll be damned, he said.

Chapter Two

The morning sun streamed through the windows, it took a little while for Tamara to remember where she was at. She smiled, she had lost her virginity in a way she could never have dreamed of, and to a real dragon as well. She sat up quickly, what had she done? Then she remembered how he had gently made love to her kissing her and holding her. A feeling of calm quiet came over her as the memories of last night flooded her mind. She heard the shower running in the room to the left. She got out of bed and peered around the corner to make sure it was Acacia in the shower. If she had learned one thing at all last night it was that the rules about privacy around these guys were not the ones she was used to. It was Acacia. She slipped into the shower beside him, just like she had seen in a few movies she had watched. Good morning, he said. Good morning, she answered, taking the soap from his hand as he offered it to her. I sent some one to bring your car here, we will see that it gets back to the company and I will pay the bill for it. Thanks, she said. Do you need for me to take you to any of your appointments in New Mexico today? No, she looked at his hard muscled body, I think I will call and quit my job. That is if you were planning to keep you part of the deal. I am, he said quickly, you can bet everything on that. Brent is calling around to get us before a judge, and you will need to go shopping for clothing, I will go with you if you like. Yes, she said, I would like that very much. Did you have any luggage or anything you needed to get from the car? If you did I'll have Brent bring it in for you. Yes, she said, he'll find all my things in the trunk. He turned off the shower and they stepped out. He gently dried her off and she slipped back into the clothes from the night before. Do you remember what I said about us mating before the circle? He asked. She had forgotten, Oh, she said. I had forgotten, that is going to be difficult for me. It is necessary or I wouldn't ask, he explained, I can't be fertile until I mate in front of the circle. How many will be there? She asked. Eleven, all dragons, all have done that before. Will they be naked also? I could have them be if that will make it easier for you. She thought a moment, if they were to be naked also it would be easier for me. She saw a look come over his face, don't ask me I don't know why. That's not a problem, it will not matter to them either way.

A thought struck her, are all of you red dragons or is there other colors? He looked into her eyes, no we come in many different colors, why? Well, she said, it's just, she hesitated. ok, you were the most beautiful creature I had ever seen. Thanks, he said. Could I see the others as dragons? Yes, they would like that, dragons like to show off their colors. Would they? She asked, surprised. You really don't understand do you? Understand what? She asked. It take us sometimes years to find a woman who after seeing us in our dragon form will even mate with us. Even then most of them do it for the money. You pay them to mate with you? Yes, and to let us keep the child. Your beautiful, I don't understand them not wanting to marry any one of you. You are the first one in my memory to ever demand to marry. She looked at him, will you be true to me? Can I bear you a child next time also? I will be true to you, and care for you, and you can bear me as many children as you can. You love me then? She asked. Yes I think I really do, I did the first time I saw you there on that cliff. He held her by the shoulders and looked into here eyes. I had thought that maybe you were interested in me like some people are into serial killers and the like, you know, mental problems. You know like. He twirled his finger about his ear. You have a self esteem problems, she told him making a face. He laughed, maybe I do, but if you knew what we went through every twelve years to mate, you might understand where I'm coming from. Maybe I would, she agreed, maybe I would. He had dressed, pulling clothes from a dresser. He wore a black knit top and black slacks. I'm so hungry, he said, I didn't eat after changing last night I'm getting weak. I'm ready to eat too, she said, let's go.

She followed him out into a hallway, then down a stairway arm in arm. What about family? He asked her. Will they be concerned for you? I only had my father, he died last year. I'm sorry. No one else? No, you can put your mind to rest, no one will miss me. Tell me about your kind, she asked, where did you come from? We really don't know, there are stories we were told, but we only know about the last eighteen hundred years, there seems to have been a disaster for our kind before that date that did away with our written history. One of the next few nights I will tell you all we know, but first I have to focus on getting you pregnant tonight. Tonight, why tonight? She queried him. It needs to be tonight, if I don't get you pregnant in the next two days it will be to late. She giggled, that sounds like fun. Oh it will be, he said. She giggled, I'm sorry I opened your flap, she said, I really thought, well you know. He laughed, I know, and It's ok, William and the others will be talking about that for the next few hundred years. No one has even attempted that on one of our kind before. It sure was big, she said, laughing again.

It is in proportion to our size. She touched his cheek, he was so modest, his black hair fell slightly over his ears, it was cut in a tussled style, she had watched him after his shower. He had run his hands through it and then had just let it dry, it really fit his face the way it lay, he was really very, very good looking. They found a breakfast ready in the dinning room kept warm on small warming trays. She was surprised how much he ate, he noticed and explained, the change uses a lot of calories, I have to replenish them. When do we go to the circle? she asked. Tonight about ten, the others will fly out, and we will mate in the forest, there is a place prepared. Don't worry, he said, seeing the look on her face, it was good last night, right? Yes, she said it was great. Well tonight close your eyes and just enjoy it, it will be no different if you just forget where you are, I will have the dragons meet us there and keep their dragon forms until I introduce you to them, that way you can see their colors. She brightened at that. That sounds good, excitement filled her face. Tamara, he said, his voice was serious. We usually mate with harlots, no one else will mate in front of a circle and with a dragon, and I say that with no reflection on you. That works best for us, we pay them and that makes them happy, they never want the trouble of children and are happy to be done with it when we take them off their hands. The fact that you want to mate because you love me will bring an excitement to the circle that has not been there in a long time. I appreciate that, and the others will really respect you for it, this will be done with the most respect that a woman could ever receive from a circle, I want you to know that, he said. I would do it for you, if for no other reason, she said. Thanks he said.

He pushed the plate from him, you ready to go shopping? Yes I am, she said rubbing her hands together. Are you really rich? Yes, he said. We will go to a city not far from here, they have a large mall, you should feel free to spend as much as you need to so you will be well dressed. As they shopped he seemed to let down any pretence he might have had. She found him witty and with a great sense of humor. He was young at heart and seemed to enjoy the small things in life. She felt very comfortable with him and had a very wonderful time. When they had returned she modeled for him for a while enjoying his smiles and hearty applause. It was twilight and she was nervous as she waited out side with him, William and Timothy had changed after they all had walked a short ways into the woods, their clothes lay on the shrubs that surrounded them as they stood waiting. William was a vibrant green color, Timothy a forest green, with lighter silver flecks that shimmered as he moved. She had walked over to them and stroked their scales, you both are gorgeous, she had told them. Why are there no female dragons? She asked Acacia. Many years ago there were, we are told a little about them in the stories handed down to us. An ancient human king came to the lair while the males were away and killed them, it is said, no female has been born since then, we do not know why. Have your kind always feared for your lives? Not always, there were times we were worshiped and reverenced. Why are there only twelve of you? There will soon be twenty four. Acacia stopped short, listen Tamara, there is something very important about that I will need to explain, I will do that tomorrow. She saw something in his eyes that made her say, it's ok, not tonight, not now, just love me Acacia. I do, he said, and I'm really happy that Brent made arraignments for us to be married tomorrow. She took his hands, yes me too.

I have to change now, he stepped back from her his raw naked body rippled in the moonlight. She stepped out of her gown also. There was the sound of the change and his large leathery wings expanded and beat the air, then his talons gently gripped her shoulders as he took flight. Her hands gripped his talons as they rose up over the trees, in a few moments he placed her in a clearing a raised platform covered in soft flowing bedding in the center. There were dragons of every one of the royal colors there. Shades of blue, green, crimson, and a few black with brightly colored specks flashing as they caught the moonlight. She turned to look at each one, and stopped when she came face to face with her love. The sound of change came all around her and she watched as Acacia became a man again. He picked her up in his arms and placed her on the raised platform and leaned down and said, close your eyes. In a moment he was over her, then she felt him penetrate her and begin to thrust. I will help you, he touched her face with his finger and that familiar tingle, though much stronger, ran up and down her spine, she was in heaven. Between each thrust she felt one hand and then another touch her shoulder and arm. Ecstasy flowed over her with each touch, and each touch brought a different tingle. She heard herself crying out and then his loud moan of release, then it was over except for the convulsive pleasure still running up her body from where they had united. He kissed her brow, then he was off her. A cover was pulled up over her and Acacia whispered into her ear, it is done you will have a dragon child.

He helped her off the platform and handed her a ski outfit, here put this on, you will be traveling by dragon this will keep you warm, it will be a good distance, but I'll be there with you so don't worry. He handed out some high protein bars to the men around him, here eat quickly, you will need the strength to change, you all know to meet at Scarborough. Tamara slipped into the ski outfit while the others ate the bars. She laughed to herself, here she was surrounded by beautiful naked men, she had fallen in love with one of them, and she was having the time of her life. She had taken the job that had required her to travel because she had been bored. She was happy, really happy and this is the first time in her life she could say that. How could she have been so fortunate to be in the right place at the right time. Each day of the last two had come with more excitement and a new adventure. Tomorrow she would get married, she was now pregnant, she had met nine new friends, would fly for the second time by dragon, and this time she was going to fly a long ways by dragon to a new house to live in. Acacia came up beside her, Alexander will take you first, he is our strongest flyer, he said, introducing him to her. He was as the other dragons, a picture of perfect form. His eyes looked a blue gray in the moonlight. A perfect smile broke over him as he took her hand and kissed it lightly as he was introduced. Brock will take you when Alexander needs rest, he should be able to finish the trip. Brock said a shy hello and kissed her hand, he was a little taller then the others, his features a little more angular, his eyes were turquoise and danced with what she thought must be mischief. I will be with you, Acacia said, but will be tending to other matters. He kissed her lightly, ready? She nodded. At a wave of Acacia's hand the sound of change was heard all around her, she felt the movement of air as wings moved to take their owners into the night sky.

She felt claws take her shoulders and she was off up and over the trees. Alexander was a powerful flyer and she moved fast through the sky on a northward line. She could see the others on all sides moving about, sometimes higher and later lower looking around at all times. After about thirty minuets she felt herself descending, Alexander dropped her gently onto the ground. Above her the others circled as Brock flew down to catcher her back up into the sky. After about ten minuets, she felt Brock's powerful wings moving them rapidly up, looking down she understood why, they were crossing a major freeway. She supposed they were doing it so as not to be seen in the lights from the cars and street lamps. After crossing the freeway they rapidly descended into a large open grassy area behind a very large estate. She felt ground under her feet and stumbled a little before catching herself.

The sound of change and a soft "sorry" caused her to turn. She smiled at Brock, his chest was heaving from the effort of carrying her, she went over and hugged him, his hard muscles tensed at her touch. I'm sorry for the rough ride, he said. No don't be sorry, she said, you were great. Brock smile at that, thanks, He said. Brock can I ask you something? He looked around him for any of the others, most of them hadn't landed as of yet. Sure, he said. It might sound stupid she said, but I noticed that all of you are so comfortable with your nakedness, I'm curious as to why? Well that's easy, he said, we are taught different then the non dragons out there. Also if you have to perform for the circle as you and

Acacia did tonight, you get over it fast. Thanks, she said. Sure he said and went of toward the house.

Acacia came up beside her, let's go inside he said, hugging her to him as they walked. You own this place also? She inquired of him. Yes and no, a company of mine has controlling interest. Will Brent be coming here as well? No Acacia said, he stays and cares for the estate we were at, we care for this one. We will need to get some rest, but tomorrow I will be filling you in on the reasons we are going to have to be doing certain things that might not make a lot of sense to you. It is something I wish I didn't have to spring on you, and I hope you will not hold it against me. Right now I just want to sleep, let's go shower you smell like sex. You do also, she said, poking him in the side. I'm sure I do, he agreed. In the shower she rubbed his back with soap, then they traded. She dried him off, then they traded and he dried her off. When they were dry they climbed into bed and sleep slammed into them like a freight train.

Tamara awoke to the sound of women arguing. She sat up listening, surely her ears were tricking her. No, it is women's voices, she could hear them arguing, that meant they must be the other dragon's mates. Acacia was no where to be found in the room, Tamara showered and dressed in record time. She was excited to have a chance to meet the other women, so she raced around getting dressed excitement filling her heart. But it was not to be as she anticipated, never had she had a disappointing moment around the dragons, today would be the first. She slipped down the hall toward the voices until she found the door to the room they were coming from. A real angry voice said, they can't keep us against our will, not in America. A softer but still bitter voice said, I don't care what I signed, I'll find a lawyer that will break the contract and then sue them. A different voice said, you two are always complaining, I knew what I was getting into and agreed to it, what's nine months for a hundred thousand dollars, beside can you imagine what one of those things can do to you if it wanted to. Me, I'll take the money and keep my mouth shut.

Still another voice said, do you believe they will pay up and let us go like they promised? I believe them, still another voice said.

Tamara open the door, hi can I come in? Tamara slipped through the door and closed it behind her not waiting for an answer. The woman with the first voice she had heard spoke to her, she was a plump dark haired woman of about thirty. Who are you? She asked glaring. I'm Acacias mate. Great, she spurted out, how did they fool you? It was the eyes, Tamara said. The forth voice said, oh hell, it was the eyes for me too, taking what Tamara had said at face value. The voice belonged to a tall shapely red head. Voice five said, it was only the money for me. This belonged to a short brunet. It was the money for all of us, if we tell the truth. This was voice number two, a medium height brunet. Tamara spoke up, it's my first day here, where do we eat? I'll take you, said voice five, getting up and heading for the door, come on, she said.

Out side of the door Tamara offered the woman her hand, I'm Tamara. Christine, the woman said shaking it. They walked down to the end of the hall, it opened into a large extravagantly furnished living area. Mirrors as tall as a dragon hung close to the floor and all but touched the ceiling. Thick oak tables, leather arm chairs and greenery was everywhere. Christine pointed to a open doorway seen through an arch and across another room. Through there, she said and turned to go back the way she came. Would you come with me? Tamara asked. I already ate, the woman said, But I'll catch you at lunch if that works. Tamara waved a small affirmation and proceeded to the doorway Christine had pointed to.

She was most of the way to the door when one of the dragons who's name she didn't know, exited walking away. Hi, she said, and placed a hand on his shoulder to get his attention. He stopped and turned back toward her. I'm sorry I haven't been introduced to you, she said extending her hand. Albert, he said. I'm Tamara, she started to say. Tamara, he said, interrupting her, taking her hand and bringing it up kissed it, I am very happy to talk with you. As I am, she said, to meet you. Albert, she said touching his arm, I'm hunting food. He smiled, right through there, he pointed through the doorway. A moment? He said catching her arm as she started to go. Sure, she said. We of the circle really appreciate what you have done for all of us, we were all sure our children were going to all die. And if I can be a little forward, how happy you have made Acacia. Thanks, she said. Is it true you made him marry you? She chuckled, yes, I told him I wouldn't have sex with out being married to him, it's what I believe in, we get married today. Albert grinned real big, you also opened his flap? Tamara really laughed, not only at the thought of what she had done, but also that it was a big deal amongst the dragons. Yes I did, but I plead ignorance. Albert was really laughing now, you know that for him to have allowed that he must have really liked you, that is an offence that in times past has gotten some female dragons in a good deal of trouble, the stories say. She leaned in to him conspiratorially, I thought I had to mate with him in dragon form. Albert howled with laughter, another head poked around the door, what's going on? Tamara stepped over to him, she extended her hand, Hi I'm Tamara. Peter, he said taking her hand softly and kissing it.

Peter was a very fair skinned man with ocean blue eyes and rusty colored hair. What did you say to him? He asked. As Albert had not finish laughing, Albert motioned to Peter, come on we have to go help Timothy, I'll tell you on the way. Peter set an almost finished glass of orange juice down on a table just inside the door and left with Albert. They hadn't gotten far when she heard them both bust up in laughter. She was smiling as she enter the room. There was no one there, she moved to the table that had chaffing dishes, some almost full, but most empty. She filled a plate and walked to another door that was in the opposite wall from the one she had come through. Opening it, she enter into another room similar to the one she had just left. There were two women there talking, and a dragon she recognized but didn't know by name. She said hi to the two women, but they ignored her. The dragon extended his hand to take hers. Roman, he said. Tamara, she said, and seated herself down beside him, noticing the two women watching her. I heard Albert and Peter, Roman said leaning in to speak low to her, I have never heard them laugh like that, I heard you talking to Albert, what the hell did you tell them? Something about a flap, she said chuckling. Oh crap, it's true then? Yes it is. Why would you? oh my, that is so funny.

The two women were whispering together, giving her strange looks. Roman leaned toward her again so the two couldn't hear them, he married you? No, but we will today, I was raised not to have sex with anyone until you were married to them, I believe in that. As far as I know a dragon has never married before, he said. He was close to her as he whispered, those two bothering you, he asked her, We could leave. She noticed a smell on his breath that she had noticed on Acacia's breath, a smell that stirred something inside her she didn't recognize at first. Then all of a sudden she understood, you produce pheromones, she said to him. He paused, we do, we secrete them. I knew that, but hadn't thought of it in a long time, you sense it? Just now with you, she said. I'm sorry he said, but when you mentioned the flap, his face reddened, well it aroused me. I didn't mean anything by it was just a reaction. I understand, no worry, she assured him. She changed the subject, why are all of you so composed all of the time? He smiled, it looks that way I suppose, it's just that almost all of us are at least an hundred years old, some much older. You get that way after a time, I suppose because you see so much, nothing much surprises you. The two women left. Don't pay any attention to them, they've been like that since they met each other, we think they like each other, if you know what I mean. Got it, said Tamara.

What is this place? Do you mean the house, Roman asked, Acacia didn't tell you? No, he said he needed to tell me something before we left last night, but he hasn't had time yet really. Are you finished eating, he asked. Yes, she said, pushing her plate a little ways away from her, all done. Let me take you to Acacia and he can explain, we tell the others, he said, lowering his voice a little, that it is a good place for them to complete their pregnancy. You, well I think he will inform you a bit farther. Roman was slim and lean. He wore tan slacks and a black pull over turtle neck. His skin color that she could see was a golden tan and his eyes were a steel gray, very mesmerizing. One moment, he said and went into a room off the hall they had been walking down. He came out with some socks and some black pull on boots. He slipped the socks and boot on as she waited and they continued walking. Tamara asked about something she had been thinking of for a while. You all are so comfortable with each other, it's like you are brothers, are you all related? Roman smiled, we are not blood related, not for a long ways back anyway, but living together and sharing so much and having to rely on each other for our very survival, that and the shared intimacy of the mating at the circle, well we ended up not having any important secrets from each other. I think that is probably what you feel. No secrets? None I know of. You know, everything about all of the dragons, Tamara said, I want to have what you all have, I like that, the openness and confidence, I believe that is why I have such a sense of belonging around you people. Well I can tell you that you have gained a good deal of respect already from each us. And you are well on your way to being a part of our lives, but there is a down side to us and that I'm sure is what Acacia is wanting to talk to you about. Please for our sakes, listen and do not judge to harshly.

They came up to an elevator, Roman keyed a code in and it opened. They went down for a floor, then the doors opened again and she walked out into a room where there was electronic equipment everywhere. All of the dragons were there. Acacia spotted her when he turned at the sound of the elevator chiming. He held up his hand and they all quieted down. This is Tamara, he said, and it is very likely everything you have heard about her is true. There were chuckles all around. I know that we are busy, but I want to take a moment to clear some things up. First, I will marry Tamara, she is my mate for ever, she has of her own free will agreed to this and is bearing my dragon child as well. She is not being compensated farther then that, I am to be true to her, and I am to take care of her needs for the rest of her life. She is my wife, by my choice and by the law, and I love her. It was quiet for a moment then they stood up a few at a time clapping until the room rang. Is there anyone of you that haven't been introduced to her, Acacia asked when the clapping had finished. Four dragons came forward, she took each hand in turn. I'm Forest, a platinum blond, his eyes were a golden color with a brown rim. He took her hand and gently kissed it. I'm Leslie, a dark skinned dragon said, his hair was black, his eyes were sea green. He also took her hand and bowing his head kissed it. Alexander, the third said, an energetic boyish blue eyed dragon, happy to meet you. He kissed her hand gently as well. Like wise, Tamara said. Now that she had seen the dragons eyes, this blue eyed one was the only one she now realized that she wouldn't know as a dragon from his eyes. The forth was stocky, hazel eyes and very mature acting. Ben, he said, kissing her hand, good to have you aboard. Thanks Ben. Acacia, clapped his hands, back to work.

He pulled her aside and planted a long hard kiss on her, good morning princess. She smiled, I guess I am a princess. You are, not that it means anything much. I have a lot to tell you but not enough time. I'll start with the important things. I'm listening she said. To lay the groundwork for what I will tell you, I'll give you a small history lesson first. A few generations before mine, there was a time that the dragons ran a mean streak. They became leaders and misused men and women until the people rebelled against it and killed all the female dragons. A short time after that a certain leader of the dragons took it upon himself to bring peace. It worked for a while, but absolute power corrupts absolutely and thing went bad. A group fought the dragons and slaughtered all but a small circle and we had only ten dragons in the world left, my grandfather and William's grandfather and some other dragons had relatives among them. All of us here are from them by human women, though none of us are really related. We lost all the female dragons and none have been born since. She was going to interrupt but he stopped her, we don't know why, he said, answering the question she was asking in her mind. A group of humans pledged to always keep our numbers down and to destroy us if they had opportunity. Each time we mate, they have attacked us, last time we lost six sons. Before that four sons. It is painful to see that, and I wish I could have told you that before you agreed to mate. They will not attack until the children are born, this time we are better prepared then they can know.

Thirty years ago we started this security business, here look at this screen. This is a satellite view of this house. We have thirty acres of property, and here is the house, he said pointing at a spot. We are surrounded by property on all sides. This is thermal imaging, it shows anyone on the property. No one but us are allowed. We have provisions enough to care for us until the boys reach puberty, if it were to come to that. We will not be allowing anymore killing of us. The leader of a circle of twenty four can access a power that you can not imagine, we will be twenty four this time, and this has not happened that we know of since the females were killed. I don't want to rule the world, nor do I want the power for my own greatness, I just want our people to be able to live without fear, that's all I ask. We are so very tired of it all. Well she said, Roman asked me to listen without judgment, I listened, Tamara said. You should know I will do what ever it takes to keep our children safe and for them to have exactly what you have said, they have the right to life as anyone else. Why has no other woman come to love your people? She asked. We have asked the same question of ourselves, we do not know. They all seem to fear us, the only thing that has any influence on people now is the money. After they see us as dragons, bribing them is the only thing that has worked. I'm going to tell you something that we hold as private. We have had to use hypnotism along with drugs to stop them from talking and breaking their contracts. We have one of the women now that we are watching very closely. Yea, I met her, Tamara said. I hope you understand, Acacia said, our kind almost became extinct, I will do almost anything to keep that from happening ever again.

Have you ever thought about going public? She asked. Yes we did, but with the way these women we are forced deal with act toward us, we are fearful, I'm sure you understand why. There was a time when the dragons stole the women we needed, raped them, acacia said, it was wrong, they were then held until they gave birth, it caused a lot of the dragon stories of old. It was after all the fair maidens that we took. Here, he said, I'll give you the code for this room, there is one more just below this one that is a safe place, when you get a chance, go and check it out. We have a job to go to right after we are married, I will be back here in two days if everything goes as planned. There are a lot of things to do around this place to have fun, just relax and find something to do to have fun. Roman and Forest will stay here and run ops, they will be in this room most of the time, give me your hand. He wrote the code to the elevator on the back of her hand, the thing to do is commit this to memory, then alcohol will take it off. As they had been talking, the others had filed out a door, now only Roman and Forest were left. Roman came over to them, everything is ready. You be careful out there please, Tamara said. I will, Acacia said, besides, we dragons have a thick hide remember. That made her smile. Come on now we leave in an hour to go before the judge, let's go get ready shall we.

Chapter Three

Tamara did find many things to do, the house was cleaned and repaired twice a week by a company, they were professional and fast, everyone was asked to go outside for a few hours. The crew of about thirty was finished in about an hour and a half and then they were all allowed to came back in. Every meal was catered, delivered to the door, the used dishes boxed and taken away at the same time. Roman told her later that every person that was to come onto the estates property to work had undergone an extensive background check that included their heritage and there could be no exceptions and no substitutes. This was the way they all would have to live for the next twelve years. So with nothing else to do she relaxed and played games and swam in the giant pool. So this was what it was like being rich, it looked like it was going to get boring. She went to check on Roman and Forest about four times a day. She would just pop in on them when ever it struck her. They always welcomed her with smiles and enthusiasm. They teased and joked and told her stories, they had lots of stories. The other women seemed to stay away from her, she didn't really care much, she had always hung with boys more then girls anyway. She was really happy when

Acacia call them to say he was going to be arriving in about an hour, she watched out the window in the hour when he was to arrive, and was rewarded with the sight of his black SUV coming up the drive. Where you and the dragons successful? Yes he said, they're cleaning up now, he said, how did you come out? I missed you, and you should get Roman and Forest to tell you some of their stories, their great. Yea, I remember those two as boys, they are both the same age you know, I actually spanked Roman once, he broke a expensive tool being stupid, I lost my temper and that was that. He did do better after that though, he's become a really great team member now, one of my best. When will the others be back, Tamara queried. Tomorrow. Who did you do this job for? Oakley Tennon. The singer, She said, surprise in her voice. Yea. He had a gig and there had been some major threats to his safety this time, his agent was really worried and insisted he have extra security. It went well, we did have one stalker we had trouble with but that was all. Acacia I need something to do if you have to be gone like this. I don't want you to misunderstand me, you have many responsibilities I know, but is there some way I can contribute to your business? Tamara said to him. I see where you are coming from, I'll see if you can do something in ops next time, ok? Thanks Acacia, that's what I was hoping for. It will help me not to worry also.

A few weeks later they had a new job, Tamara had been trained it the monitoring of the communication consul. Each day she monitored the talk going on between the crew and was in close quarters with Brock and Peter as it was them that stayed behind for ops support. She felt like she had a job and was useful, the dragons were to be gone for over a week and it passed in a flash and she was hugging Acacia again. Was that better? he asked. Yes hearing your voice every day and being so busy made it pass fast. This is a very interesting job, I would never had imagined. It is a good occupation, he agreed, and it gives us a reason to have all of this equipment, it cuts down on people getting nosey. Do you miss being with the other women? He asked her. No they don't really seem to want me around and I like the boy's games better. Acacia laughed, you are a very interesting person Tamara, very refreshing. Speaking of refreshing, why don't you get refreshed and we will eat and then hit the sack early. I'm two months and a half, five more months and we have to cut it out for a while. I can't wait for him to be born, they killed my last three sons. I'm so sorry, Tamara said, I didn't know. It's all right, I know we're much better prepared this time. It is so lucky we are twelve, because double that is twenty four. Why is twenty four so important? Tamara asked. Well we really don't understand why but at twenty four and then at forty eight we have a power that we can wield against our enemies and virtually control them with thought. It is some thing I will have to learn how to do, and as far as we understand, only I as leader will be able wield it, but it will make us almost invulnerable. We get it as soon as all the children reach puberty. I will worry until then.

How do you know about this power? There is a book written by a dragon about six hundred years ago he speaks of it as if was common place in dragon history. His book has been used and has been correct before. I'll tell you something, he said getting very serious. I feel responsible for the loss of many of the boys, I didn't take my place as a leader to heart and went about the protection of the circle with less then my best, but no more. I am going to take care of us all and make us strong again. She took his hand, I believe you, and I want to have a part with you and help. You promise to let me help? I will be happy to let you help in any way I find that you can, I need all the help I can get. She put her hand on his shoulder when she saw the look of grief on his face, it must have been really hard. Dragons died because of me, some were just children, the rest of the dragons almost left me. She could see his pain reflected in his eyes. It's all right now though? Yes, but it is still hard, the reason the others are here is because William vouched for me. They trust you now I can see it for my self, she said. Yea we have all really come together and it has been good for ten years now. They have all of their trust in me now and I will not let them down.

The next morning Tamara felt like the luckiest person to have ever live. Acacia was like a stallion and she was satisfied completely. Today they were to spend all the day just messing around the estate doing whatever they wanted to. He had given her a credit card, and shown her a computer in ops she could access the net from. He told her to get some nice things, he was going to take her out to a restaurant. She had protested she was already showing. Good, he had said, I can show off. She had nibbled his ear while they had showered the night before and received a new experience of the power of his pheromones again, and that was how the night had started. Later in the day Ben called him away for a short time, so she went to ops to do some shopping. She was in ops when they both came through the door talking. I can't do anything with her, Ben was saying, she never shuts up and threatens us all the time she is talking. Tamara knew they were talking about the mouthy dark haired woman she had talked to in that room her first morning. They walked across the room and into the elevator still talking. She could see Ben was clearly at his wits end, she heard him say, you know what we used to do to these kind. Yes, but we have chosen a different way now, and the door closed.

Tamara decided to shop later, she hadn't seen any of the other women in about a week as she had made sure not to go where they might be. Now she was hunting them, she looked in about five rooms before finding one of them. Where is Susan? She asked the brunet that sat in a chair reading a book. She is in the spa all the time, check there. Tamara didn't even know there was a spa, so she asked directions. Getting the directions she made her way there. She open the door to find nine of them enjoying many of the amenities, half of them naked. She spotted Susan and went up to her. I need to talk to you. What would a person like you want to say to me? Six years of her helping her father restore old vehicles came to play right at that moment. A hard right to Susan's mouth knocked her back and she tumbled over a planter. Tamara was on her as the other scattered, staring in disbelief. Grabbing her by her hair and holding her face close she said, you have a agreement with those men and they have done you nothing but good. My advise to you is shut your mouth and spend the remainder of your contract staying quiet and enjoy yourself. When your contract expires and they pay you, forget this ever happened and go on with your life. She put her mouth to her ear, if you do not, I will hunt you down and take at least a day to kill you, do you understand? Susan nodded her head yes. Do you believe me? She nodded again. Good, because I'm like you I have nothing, and if I were to spend a few years in prison because I killed you, it would be more then worth it. Don't let me see or hear you again. Susan nodded her head again, tears in her eyes. Tamara let go of her and turned to the others. My advice to all of you is do what I told her.

Out side the door her legs shook, she leaned against the wall for support, took a few deep breaths and made for the ops, she wasn't sure what had come over her, but she did know she wasn't going to let anyone ruin what she was coming to love. She stopped at the door where the woman was that gave her directions and sticking her head in said, I found her, thanks. The woman acknowledged her. Tamara was in ops in no time, she needed to finish her shopping. An hour later, Acacia found her and asked if she was hungry. Sure, she answered. Let's go eat, I've been so busy today I haven't had much time except to get a bite or two.

The next time Acacia had to leave, he was going to be away for a week. William and Alexander was in Ops. Tamara manned the communications center, it was extraordinarily busy as there were three separate teams working in unison a small distance from each other. The traffic on the radios very was intense, she enjoyed the pace and later when she was getting coffee, William complimented her on her handling of the com. Thanks William, that is a high compliment when it is coming from you. William chuckled and said, did Acacia tell you I didn't really trust you? No, no one told me, it's in those dragon eyes. You hide it well but I can see you don't really trust me, even right now you don't trust me. Your smart, I'll give you that, he said. Well you know William, you never flinched in doing what Acacia asked concerning me and even when he let me in here, you kept a very professional attitude. I have to say you did better then I would have if I had been in your shoes. I really respect that. Now let me put your mind to ease, something I probably could have done if you would have come to me with your concerns in the first place. She had gotten started and now she ploughed on. First, do you really believe that I would have risked my life by hanging myself off a cliff side, hoping some dragon flying around out there, might out of the goodness of his heart, come swooping down to save me? Really? And what would I have done if he decided that it was better if he didn't expose himself, then what? I'm sure you checked my background already, did you find any discrepancies? What about my appointments? Were they real or not? Just because I fit into your lifestyle so well, you are sure I'm a spy? Have you thought that maybe I really care and respect your kind, even though no one in a long time has? She was breathing hard. Alexander had listened, as her voice had risen with her anger, he came and stood beside them and was listening. Are you finished? William asked. After a moment, she answered, I suppose I am. I agree with you, he said, and up until I heard what you did to Susan I was suspicious, but I believe you now, and I was going to tell you that until you started in on me. Tamara felt herself blush, she felt bad. I'm sorry, she said. No problem, he extended his hand, truce? She took it, truce.

Alexander ventured, we really need someone on Communication. Tamara rushed to her station, sorry! She said to the voice that was calling her name. At the coffee bar in ops,

Alexander looked at William, I believe her. Yes, me too, but it is so damned convenient for her to come along just when we needed a woman to save our unborn children. Then on top of that she wanted to marry Acacia and willingly bear his children. Maybe fate has really smiled on us for once, Alexander proclaimed. She's just to good to be true, William countered, but with no real conviction. I'll take it even if it seems to good, Alexander said, look how happy Acacia is, look how he is handling the jobs, it has been over a hundred years since I've seen him like this. William just nodded his agreement and walked out. She's damn good at the com, he heard Alexander say as he left.

Chapter Four

She always anticipated Acacias return home with excitement, he would always come to see her first and he would bring her a little something he had bought, then that night he would be furiously wild in bed. The passion of those nights when he came back would remain in her heart always. She sighed at the thoughts, as she waited by her favorite window, the one that overlooked the drive coming in. There he was, a black SUV pulled up the drive stopping in front of one of the six garage doors. His slim figure stepped out into the sun, she ran to hug him, her sun dress flowing out behind her. His smile for her made her so proud to be with him. After their kiss she turned to the others standing by and shook their hands greeting each one by name. She had spent one day learning each ones name by associating it with the color of their eyes, There was nothing more arresting then a dragons eyes. She had thought back through her life, and had asked herself if she had ever seen a dragons eyes before. If she had, she was sure she would have remembered it. Forest leaned in and spoke to her, really good job at the com this trip. Thanks, she smiled at him. I mean it, he said with sincerity. She watched Forest and Roman leaving together, there was something between those two and she was going to find out what on the down low. She placed her hand into Acacia's back pocket as the made their way to the house. I'm starved, he said, did you leave anything for me? I have a plate for you and me in our room. You can clean up and then we'll eat. In their room she watched him as he stripped, she rubbed his dragon skin, loving that particular feel that it had. She followed him to the shower. We are going to do a night flight tomorrow night, he asked her, you want to come along? What exactly is a night flight? We all get together and spend a few hours flying, we do it at night so we are least likely to be seen. The others don't care if I come? No, they want you to come, I don't know exactly how you did it, but they have a great deal of respect for you. I love them all, you know, she said, not the same way I love you but it is love. And I feel sorry for them, after all the humans have did to them. Also I respect them, and you especially, because all of you have forgiven us. I would love to be there when you night fly. Good, he said, kissing her on her forehead.

She waited for him to shower, when he exited, she dried him off, savoring a close view of him and the feel of his skin. How do the dragons keep such a composure, she asked still amazed. We have practice, all but two of us are over an hundred years old. I can tell you, but not really explained it, he said. It's seductive you know, she said, licking her lips. Really? he asked. Yea, she continued, it gives me a safe feeling, that calm cool collected, all knowing look, each one of you have. Is that good? He asked. Yes, very good, all warm and fuzzy good, she said. Now where's that meal? He asked looking around. Over by the patio doors. She watched the sinews and muscles of his body move as he strode across the room. He sat naked in one of the chair by the doors, the sun shinning on his skin, causing it to sparkle as only a dragons skin could. She sat on his lap and fed him, kissing his cheeks in between bites. I'm seven months, she said patting her belly, we could do a sonogram and check it out. No, sorry doll, he explained, no doctors. Oh, yea forgot, Tamara said, Then who is going to deliver the babies? Leslie is a fully trained doctor, Acacia said, he just didn't get licensed. He has delivered many babies, and keeps up on his training. She had finished feeding him, she liked babying him his first night back from a job, after that he was usually busy getting things ready for the next job. Even at that, he always had time for her, but she stayed out of the way as much as possible. As she was in charge of the com, she was included in all the briefings, this kept her in the know of what was going on, which made her feel far more comfortable.

What do you want to do, Acacia asked her, we have the rest of the day together, you want to do anything in particular? Tamara thought on it a while. I would like to sit in the spa if no one is there, my back has started to hurt from carrying the baby, I thought the spa might help. Then a short swim and a movie if you wouldn't mind. He stood up and walked over to the closet and found him a pair of swim trunks, he wore the tight kind and she like to see him in them. She slipped into a bikini and they pulled robes over themselves and went to the spa to see if it was occupied. The tiles were wet around the spa but no one was there. Looks like we lucked out, he said, throwing his robe off and stepping in. She followed him and let out a sigh as the hot water began to ease the pain in her back. He rubbed her back for a while and then they both leaned back into the depressions made into the sides and relaxed. How often do the dragons fly? Tamara asked. As a circle, about once every other month, he answered, we would like to more often, but it doesn't work out. Sometimes as a small group, like two, three or four, we do it on the spur of the moment. Like when you rescued me? She asked. He turned and smiled at her, yea, like that. It must be heavenly to fly like that. It is special, and exhilarating. It refreshes the soul. How far can you fly before resting? She asked. Alexander has flown in a test fly almost four hundred miles. We clocked him at almost one hundred miles an hour, in a short burst. Where do you fly to test at? We go to the desert because there are few to no people out there. We will take the kids out there for their first flights. Dragons lead such a great life, full of excitement, she said. It's a lot better now then it used to be. Stupid as it may have been, we used to not work together. What pulled you all together? She prompted him. Actually it was who, and it was William, he came to me and we worked out a plan, one by one we pulled the dragons we could find together, we have prospered ever since. William loves you like a brother, she told him, he is very protective of you. Yea, he smiled at her, he told me what happened. I told him not to worry with you, he kept saying it was to good to be true. You made an impression on him that day, he will be as protective of you from now on just like he is to me.

Tamara changed the subject, how are all the other women doing? Well Leslie just did checkups on the ones that are eight months, everything looks good. Three are going to be eight months sometime in this month, including you. He had to turn Alice's baby around or it would have been breach, but that went ok. We were having some trouble with Susan and it looked like we were going to have to take some drastic measures with her, then one day she just quit giving us trouble. Tamara smiled to herself, so William hadn't told what he knew, she was grateful. Let's swim she said, I'm getting hot, are you ready? He stood up, then helped her up, they walked out the double doors into the night. Acacia stretched while Tamara lower herself into the pool. He dived in at the opposite end then coming up out of the water beside her. We will not be taking on any more jobs until the boys are all one year old. Some of the circle will be taking vacations, some will be going to training, some will go to make purchases for the business etcetera. Some are going to see if they can find someone to be their wife, he chuckled. I'm staying here with you and my son. She hugged him there in the water, the sun setting behind the hills gave the water a red tinge. Acacia I don't ever want this to end, I wish there was some way I could never grow old like you. We are planning to see if we can find a way to do that, but I expect it will not be soon if ever, that's a hard thing to do, other scientist are working on it. We do have one thing in our favor though, we have dragons to study and see if we can find out what keeps us from aging. Even though you don't, she added, as she caressed his face, I wouldn't change my luck or my state for nothing. And concerning finding something to do, I do have an idea where to start.

It's early, I don't want to retire now, he said. We still have a movie to watch, she reminded him, nibbling on one of his nipples. Well then, let's get dressed and let's watch it in the theatre that way it will seem like a real one, he said, I haven't watched a movie in the theatre in over a year, he walked up the steps out of the pool. He loved her, she was very sure, but there was something about him that still made him seem far away. So much history she assumed, so many years, so many things, so much responsibility, all of it she didn't share with him. They selected a movie from the rack that was in the foyer, and going inside they were surprised to find it occupied. Roman was slipping a disc into the player Forest was seated in the center recliner in the seating area. Roman turned at the sound of the door closing, I just slipped in Terminator, he said apologetically. Good Acacia said, is it ok if we watch it with you? he asked turning to look at Forest. They both agreed it would be good to have company, Acacia took a seat below them and he and Tamara cuddled up. As the speaker began blasting the opening salvos from the machines guns she asked him, do you know about those two? Yes I do know, how did you know? It's obvious. She said, shrugging. Well maybe to you, he said, but as far as I know only myself and William know, they have been really discrete, we only know because we caught they once by accident.

They were almost through the movie when the doors opened and Brock came in, he went to Acacia, Elisabeth has started labor a little early, Leslie wants you there he needs your advice. Come with me please, he asked Tamara, she motioned her agreement. They followed Brock as he wound his way to the infirmary. Upon seeing them, Leslie pulled them aside and explained. She is half a month premature, and she has started full labor. We can care for the child and he will be fine. So with your leave I want to let her continue with the labor, that would be best I think. Acacia agreed, most of the women want to get out of here as soon as possible. Can I go see her, asked Tamara, she looks scared and all you have are men here, she probably would like the company of a woman. That would be great, agreed Leslie, we have wanted a midwife to help, it has never seemed to work out yet.

Tamara went in to the young woman. Elisabeth right? The woman clasped her hand like a drowning person. I'm Tamara. She nodded her head, yes I know. I was there when you talked to Susan. Tamara grinned at that. Well Elisabeth, Tamara said rolling her eyes toward the dragons, have they been treating you all right? The dragons have been good to me, Elisabeth said, but I have never had a child before and I'm a little nervous. I know how you feel, mine turn is coming and I'm a little nervous already. Really Elisabeth said, visibly calming down. I'm here to stay for as long as it takes, Tamara comforted her, I also know they have your best interest in mind, I know that for sure. It is in everyone's best interest for you to complete the contract and take the money and make a life for yourself. The girl relaxed even farther, thanks, she said, when your scared a lot of stupid thing come into your head. She cried out in the pain of another contraction. I know honey, Tamara said, I know. In the wisdom of their kind, the dragons all waited outside the room leaving Tamara to handle Elisabeth, Leslie coming only periodically to check her vitals. He had given her instructions on what to do and what to watch for and then watched from a distance. Tamara looked at the clock, three hours had passed, it was just past midnight and now she motioned for him to come, as the time was getting close and Elisabeth was past caring who was there.

Delivery was a sweet high of a job well done, with the sweet relief of rest after fatigue. All the dragons celebrated at the bar in the library, they toasted Brock on his new fatherhood, and asked after his child's name. Acacia explained to her that Brock was from the last generation and was one of the two dragons under one hundred. Tamara couldn't tell as they all looked to be twenty or a little older. After thanking Tamara profusely Leslie, suggested that she get some rest as she was only a few short weeks away from labor herself. Acacia picked her lovingly up in his arms to applause from the dragons, took her to the shower in their room and helped her remove her clothing. She showered, and he put her to bed slipping in beside her.

Morning came to the sound of the shower running and the sun starting to light the east sky. Tamara slipped out of bed and went to peek into the shower at him. When he saw her, he said, "good your up," We're leaving in about an hour or so to drive to the desert, you should start getting ready. She stretched and yawned and slipped out of her night things and into the warm stream of the second shower head. Did I get the right temperature? He asked. Yea, she said, hot just like everything else about you. She started by washing her cinnamon colored hair, and had rinsed it, when she felt his strong hands washing her body taking a long time as he rubbed her tummy and spoke to the baby for a while then he kissed her and climbed out. She finished in a short time and he was waiting with a towel for her, helping her dry off. Wear something comfortable but not to thick, we will be taking some warmer outer wear. He was dressing in his customary black on black. She understood now why he wore certain clothing, they were easy to get into and out of. They were a rowdy bunch, as all of them except Leslie piled into two waiting Hummers, Acacia and Tamara selecting the back seat of one. Tamara really enjoyed the mood of the dragons as they celebrated life, the coming dragon children, and just being boys. Acacia set with her, seeming content to just hold her and periodically kiss her somewhere.

By five they were getting close to their destination and about seven they pulled off onto a side road. We bought this property about one hundred and eighty years ago, right after we came together as a full circle. We were not wealthy and pooled our money so we could have a place to fly, Acacia said, I know this terrain like the back of my hand. They all unloaded and set up tables, and a tent for her to keep her out of the elements. They ate a slow and leisurely a dinner they had brought from the caterers, and told stories from the recent past. As the last of the sun slipped below the horizon, they stood in a circle and stripped down. They all seemed to forget that she was here, they seemed totally enthralled in the thing they about to do. Acacia had given her a set of night vision binoculars, she would use them after they were airborne so she could see them in the night sky. She watched as William counted one, two, three, then the now familiar whoosh and the mist that surrounded them and eleven dragons stood where the men had stood. It was an incredible sight, even in the fading light their skin caught what light was left, the sparkling colors were breathtaking. One by one they launched skyward, their great wings stretched and beat against the air stirring the shrubs and sand, the air causing their wings to bulge each time the wing came down. Acacia had told her they would begin by scouting the area looking for anyone that might have gotten themselves onto the property. Then they would fly for the fun of it. As the last one of them flew out of her sight, she place the binoculars to her eyes and watched as they flew acrobatically amongst the stars. She envied their gift and the freedom it must be to fly under the heavens so free. From time to time, one of them would fly low over her to do a summersault and shoot away. She sat there at peace, she had an idea now where her life was going, and who she was traveling with.

A few hours later, one by one they landed, changing just it time to land on their feet in human form. They would then fall to the ground their chest heaving from the exertions of the flight. She brought each one a bottle of water and handed it to them as they lay there. Acacia was forth to land, and she watched him in the lantern light as the sweat glisten on his heaving chest until the others had all landed. They dressed and packed and then it was the drive home. Pheromones and the musky smell of men, the hum of their excited talk lulled her into a deep and peaceful sleep.

They had no more then entered the door when Leslie came to them, another one of the girls in going into labor. Is she early? No, not this one, this is Peter's woman, he was the first in the circle. I'll get a shower and be right there, Tamara said, What's her name? Her name is Joan. Tell Joan I'll be there in just a few minuets for me. He nodded his agreement and she rushed to their room for a shower. Acacia came in behind her, you don't have to be there for every delivery if you don't want to, he said. I know, but if it makes it easier on them and Leslie I would like to, she said as she entered the shower. He stepped in behind her, I'm sure the women would appreciate it and I know Leslie will, he never has wanted the position of delivering the children, but I can not trust anyone from the outside. It's settled then, Tamara said. Yes he said hugging her. William is right though, you are to good to be true. Thanks love, she said, kissing him on the cheek. As with Elisabeth, Joan was more frightened then anything. When Tamara stepped into her room, she visibly relaxed, and after Tamara had spoken with her a while, she seemed ready for the birth. Seven hours later, another dragon boy was in the nursery. Acacia had asked Tamara to be there when he settled the contract with Elisabeth. Try to see if you can tell if we are likely to have any trouble from her, he asked, also if you can see if there might be a better way to handle them as we send them away.

When Elisabeth came into the room, Acacia spoke to her about the terms of her agreement, and emphasized the part to keep their transaction confidential. Acacia paid her in cash giving it to her in a small leather pouch and warning her to not deposit it, or she might bring the attention of the IRS to her. Instead he explained, put it in a safe deposit box and use it slowly supplementing other income. She was agreeable to all they said, and then she left with their thanks for everything. Acacia and Tamara watched as she waved from the taxi Acacia had waiting for her. She will keep our agreement I'm quite sure, Tamara told him. They didn't know then, but in one week they would only have two undelivered babies. Tamara was relaxing by the pool when her turn came. She was two weeks early, she knew that because she had spoken to Leslie at her check up the day before and he had told her then she had two more weeks. The pain shot through her again, making her gasp. The thought, Susan was supposed to be next to give birth, rocketed through her mind. That was the way it was supposed to be. She worked her way to standing position and made for the house, Brock came out a door to her left and she called for him. He smiled a big smile when he understood her dilemma. What is so humorous? she snapped at him, a pain hitting her at the same moment. Acacia will be so happy, he said. Good, help me to the infirmary and go get this happy person. Right, he said, and picked her up in his arms, as she screamed in surprise.

Chapter Five

The pain hit again, it hit like a freight train and she screamed. Another woman screamed beside her, it was Susan, they had brought her into the infirmary a half an hour after she had gotten there. Acacia had been hovering over her for five hours, getting glares from Susan that he was much to excited to see. Leslie was saying push, she could hear his voice through the fog of pain, she pushed and the searing pain, then almost no pain, and the cry of a baby. She gasp out, is he ok? But no one answered her, they were staring at the baby. She panicked, let me see him, she screamed. As if shaken from a daze, Leslie brought the baby over into her sight. It's a girl, he said, a baby girl. She looked down at the baby, then covered her mouth with her hand. Is it a dragon girl? Leslie raised the little arm into the bright lights. Even Tamara could see the sparkle to the skin, she whispered, Oh Acacia, amazement filling her tone, a dragon girl.

The news spread so fast, she was shocked at how soon all the dragons were in the room filling it, each taking turns to see her baby. What is her name, William asked? Tamara looked at Acacia, they hadn't talked about female names. He looked to her for a response, she motioned for him to give her a name. Her name is Annabelle, Acacia said. Annabelle, Tamara cooed. Susan delivered about thirty minuets later and they had moved her into her own room. All of a sudden Alexander spurted out, it is love. They all stopped talking, looking at him. What? Acacia said. Think about it, he said, that's the only difference, she loves you. He went on, I was asking myself why a dragon girl, the only difference is love. They all understood what he was trying to say, and nodding agreement. We never thought of that, Alexander went on. Remember Isabel? Isabel was the only woman that loved one of us in what six hundred years, Alexander said. But she died, she died before we had time for the circle, remember? They were all nodding their heads in agreement. Brock said, I can get a woman to love me, we all can. Acacia cautioned, we are not positive about this, so let's move slowly ok? They all nodded agreement to that also. Tamara looked from face to face, it was obvious that they wouldn't be waiting for long though. There was a look of hope on each of them and it was gong to take more then a cautionary word to take it away from them. It was then that she understood how this business of having to bribe women to be with them and bear their children was weighting heavy on them. It was plain to her even through the calm exterior, that they each wanted a family and the things it brought. It was also plain to her that it was a special bond that allowed them to be so happy for one of the circle when one of them found that happiness, and to not be jealous of each other. She set her mind right then to see that each of them would have a family, and to do all she could toward that end. Twelve years from now their would be twenty four new dragons born, and as many of them girls as she could make happen. She already had some ideas.

Tamara stood beside Acacia as he went back over the agreement with Susan, she kept giving Tamara an angry look. One hundred thousand is not enough, she argued. It is what you agreed to and we will not be blackmailed by you or anyone else. Acacia had been trying to get her to give her word not to cause them any trouble for almost an hour, but she had skirted around the subject and doing that by arguing about the details. Give me a moment alone with her, Tamara said. Acacia looked at her for a moment, then said, I'll be right out side. When the door closed behind him Tamara asked, what is it you really want?

To her surprise Susan turned red in the face. Susan didn't answer for a moment then said, I like Ben. It was Tamara's turn to be shocked. Does he like you? Tamara asked. There was water in Susan's eyes, I don't know, she said, I hope he does. I want to stay here, but none of them has asked me. Tamara went over to her and hugged her, why didn't you just say so? Tamara asked. Would you have? Susan answered vehemently? Would you want to be where no one wanted you? No I guess I wouldn't, your right. Susan looked into her eyes, you understand? Yes, of course, I'm in love with Acacia, why wouldn't I understand? But he loves you back, she countered. Did you give Ben a chance to love you back? A chance, Susan said, we went to dinner and he brought me to meet Acacia. They showed me they were dragons, I agreed to their terms, we signed the contract and then the circle, and I only saw him a few times after that. When was I supposed to find out if he liked me? I see, Tamara said. Ok now listen to me, Tamara said. These men have experienced a lot of rejection. It probably never entered his mind that you were in the least bit interested. Tamara took her by the shoulders and looked deep into her eyes, will you stay here and give me a few days? Yes, Susan said, if they will let me. But what are you going to do? You leave that to me, you go see your baby and spend a few days resting, I'll come talk to you soon. Ok, She said nodding. Do you trust me? Tamara asked her. After a moment she nodded yes. Ok go, and don't worry ok? Ok, she agreed.

After she had left, Acacia came back in. This is very interesting Tamara said. Go on, Acacia said. She told him all that transpired between her and Susan just then. Do you know how Ben feels about any of this? No, Acacia said. He may not have any idea. Will you find out quietly? She asked, I believe she really likes him. I can do that, Acacia said. If he really doesn't love her and it turns out to be a mess, it will be worse then this mess, she cautioned. Yes, he said I see what you are saying, I'll do this right, trust me, he said, besides it would solve one of our problems wouldn't it? Thanks, she kissed him, if this turns out good, it will be a very good start for the dragons. Yes it would, he agreed.

The next day in the afternoon, Acacia came to her in the nursery. I've been looking for you, Leslie told me you were down here, he said kissing her passionately. I can't get enough of looking at her, Tamara said. Yea, I moved a crib into our room, we can bring her there with us, he said touching Annabelle's cheek. Oh thanks, she said hugging his neck. My pleasure, he said, she brings a new beginning for us all. Now about Susan. I had William ask Ben how he had felt about her. He said he really liked her until she had watched him change, after that she had been cold to him, so he had left her alone. Well what if we ask him if we should let her stay, tell him she asked to get to know him better. Ok, he said, I have learned to trust your people skills so I'm in. Good, ask him as soon as possible please so I can go tell Susan, get her out of suspense. I'll do it now. She picked up Annabelle and covered her with a blanket, I'll be in our room getting her settled in. When she arrived at their room a bright pink ribbon crossed the door, a pair of scissors were leaning by the doorjamb. She retrieved the scissors and cut the ribbon. Inside, the most beautiful crib stood by the bed. It was carved oak with a canopy, a gorgeous quilted covering adorned the mattress. She placed Annabelle in the crib covering her, she didn't even stir. Acacia came in quietly after just a few minuets, he was very interested, he said referring to Ben. Can you get him to the bar in let's say half an hour, she asked. Probably, he said. Good, give me a second to ask Susan and I'll be back. Ok, he said, but he was already distracted watching Annabelle as she slept. She went to find Susan, since it was late she checked her room first. Not finding her she decided to go to the dinning room. Passing through the library, she found her at the bar. Hey, she greeted her. Hi, she said back, without much enthusiasm. Ben is interested in getting to know you better, Tamara told her, excitement in her voice.

Susan brightened, what do I do? Well expect him here in a few minuets. Susan straightened up and checked her makeup in the mirror over the bar. Tamara went and told Acacia to have Ben come to the bar. Back at the bar Tamara made small talk with Susan until Ben came into the room, excusing herself she headed back to her room and Acacia. Acacia was laying naked across the bed still watching the sleeping Annabelle. She laughed at him, you act as if you have never seen a baby before. She is so beautiful, he said grinning from ear to ear, look at her just sleeping so peaceful. Do I have competition? Tamara feigned worry. There is no competition for you in the whole wide world. Get off, she said. You can't fool me, slick willy, she rubbed her hand down his back. Look what you gave me, he said. A whole new life, and things I had thought impossible have happened. I didn't do all this by myself, Tamara told him, it was all of us. That is partly true, he agreed.

Are you coming to bed, he asked. Let me shower, she told him. There was aloud knock at the bedroom door. Acacia jumped up and Annabelle started to cry softly. Acacia went to the door, Alexander was there. William wants you to come to ops, there has been a movement on perimeter, could be nothing but he wants you to come to ops if you would. I'm coming, Tamara said when Acacia started pulling on clothes. Alexander will you watch Annabelle? Sure he said. She should be asleep in a few moments, she told him. They hurried to ops, and found William intently watching a screen. It was here, he pointed to a place in the southwest corner of the estate. There was a heat signature the right size to be a person. It moved onto the property and the computer sounded the alarm, then it blinked out. You mean the signature moved out of the property, asked Acacia? No, said William, it winked out as if it became to cold for the sensors to pick it up. The trouble is we don't know if it left the property or what. I'll replay the footage and you see what you think. They all watched as a red signature moved across the line that signified the border of the property. Then moved back toward the line then winked out. Has any trip wires sounded or perimeter beams been tripped? No, none. Get us a satellite view. William turned to a computer and typed. After a little time he had something on a screen. Enhance the area where we saw the image. There, acacia said, pointing to what looked to Tamara like a dot. Follow this image to image. William typed commands into the computer. The dot moved in toward the house a short time, then moved perpendicular to the property line. After a little it moved back across the property line and away. What do you make of that? It's either a bum, or someone testing or security. A bum can't make our heat sensors blind, and if someone is testing the security, how did they make our infrared blind, what did they use? Put someone here in ops with who ever is on duty all night, Acacia told William, and tomorrow look for an upgrade for those night vision cameras. Tamara and Acacia bid William good night and they went back to their room. Relieving Alexander and thanking him, they both showered and then climbed into bed.

When they went to the dinning room the next morning, Ben and Susan were sitting by each other laughing and talking. William came in and Acacia was updated on the night events. Nothing more had happened in the night and at daybreak they had inspected the ground in the area. Foot prints all right, William told them, not a bum's either, looked like dress shoes. Acacia asked himself out loud, why would anyone in dress shoes be there, there's no road for half mile or so. Let's put a dog out there and a remote release, William said, the dog can chase him down giving us time to get out there, we could use a quiet cage. Acacia leaned toward Tamara, she had asked him to explain to her what a quiet cage was. It is a cage that keeps the sound of the dog from being heard by the target, one of Peter's ideas. He comes up with some good ideas every so often. Susan caught Tamara's eye and mouthed a thank you. No problem, she mouthed back. Looks like we have a problem solved in Ben and Susan, Tamara whispered in Acacia's ear.

Tamara spent a good deal of time in the nursery each day hugging and holding the babies. Leslie spent a great deal of time there also, and the others took turns watching and caring for them. After a few days they moved them to a room on the second floor that overlooked the spacious rear grounds. They each had a crib and some small toys. She noticed that the dragons were all adept at the soothing and handling of the children and cared for them with the skill that could only come with practice and love. Susan and Ben had taken Cameron their child to be with them in a room they now shared. Susan cared for Cameron with much fuss and for Ben with tender care. Tamara was worried a little for Acacia, he had been tense since the intruder, but there had been no other incident for three days, so now he seemed to be convinced that it was a testing of their security and response. It was cold out now, winter having fully set in, much different then the early spring days when they had first met. Tamara had watched Acacia fall in love with Annabelle more and more each passing day. A session of him playing with her before they retired for the night was always followed with his wild passionate love making to her. She was amazed at his physical abilities in the bed. One evening after watching Albert feed the babies she, she slipped out of the nursery and in to feed Annabelle. Acacia was there, a bottle in hand having just finished feeding her. We are warming the pool tonight, he said upon seeing her, we do a midnight swim once each winter. I would have told you earlier, but it all was decided in the last few hours. They all wanted to have the swim tonight, you and Susan are invited, we will move the babies to the library so we can check on them from time to time. He held up his hand, forestalling her agreement. It is a naked only event, and it has been that way for over twenty years. There will also be drinking, tonight and New Years are the only two nights we drink. I'm coming, she said. Good the boys will be pleased, he said, they really enjoy these parties.

Chapter Six

The pool was filled with raucous laughter and naked bodies, Tamara understood that this was a day that they set aside to forget all the responsibilities, and just have fun. They did just that. It was wild and no game was turned down. No one was self conscious, about anything, they just had fun. She was pushed into the pools warm water so many times that she had lost count. Warm naked bodies had been shoved against her and had tackled her, and she had tackled even more. They were in and out of the pool as much as any teenagers would be. Two hours later she lay beside Acacia on a towel, the cold air hitting her body. He cupped her breasts in his hands and kissed her. Let's take Annabelle and go to bed he said. Let's go. As they passed through the library she asked him who is going to take care of the babies? Brock said he would, Brock came in drying himself off. Don't worry, he said,

I saw you two leave and I came to take care of them, you two go to bed. Tamara smiled her thanks and picking up Annabelle, they headed for bed. She patted Acacia's rear as they moved into the elevator, you dragons have a interesting life style. We had to find things for us to do to keep our sanity. We usually go on a ski trip early in the year, but we all decided to stay with the children this first year, so we will be doing the things we usually do at the compound. This is the first time we had girls at our swim party, it was nice. A few of the boys want to go to a bar in town and see if they might get as lucky as Ben and me, but I would rather they go farther from the compound then that. Also I want them to wait a year, or until we have had time to address better protection for the children. I think it better if no new faces were introduced into the environment. That is true, Tamara agreed, but the dragons would do better with companionship of the female kind. You said you can do extensive background checks? Yes, he answered. Then how about one at a time with a thorough background check. I'll think about it, he said yawning. He slipped into bed while she fixed Annabelle a bottle, and was asleep when she finished feeding her. She looked down at his peaceful slumber and was so thankful for her life this past year.

Two days later he told her Alexander was going to try find a girl in San Diego. That's what, one hour from here? She was surprised they would need to go that far. Hour and a half, he said. He is going to try to find a girl that has few attachments, one that he likes. If he does, he will ask her to come stay for a weeks visit. If she will, we were hoping you could help her get comfortable with us. What if she ends up not liking him? Well, we think that if one of the other dragons like her, then we will have him try. Isn't it early? You can't mate for twelve more years. We are going to offer her companionship, and a place to call home, and nothing more to see how we come out, you know as a trial, see if it has possibilities. Tamara agreed with their logic, as a trial, she said. Acacia nodded his head. When is he going? Tomorrow, Peter is going with him for protection, we don't usually travel alone you never know what will happen and we really can't afford any big problems now.

That night they had another intruder, the dog was loosed, but he came back after they had heard him barking for a half an hour. The next day they found a set of prints and the dogs prints following them. A patch of burnt grass made them conclude that the intruder had set off some sort of smoke grenade to stop the dog from following, as the tracks led off from the burnt patch to the perimeter of the property. Some one is watching us, said Timothy. He would do better if he used a satellite, William said. Maybe, but this person may not have access to one. A peeping tom? Leslie asked. Maybe, Acacia agreed, plenty of nudity here, could be just a peeping tom. What about the heat signature fading? Maybe wrapped himself in a cold garment with a hood. What about the burnt area, William asked, A flare? Could have been, Acacia said, but there should be ashes, let's go look at the satellite pictures. They watched the figure as it moved in toward the house, stopped for a little moment then ran. That was when the dog was released, William said. The figure ran for a distance, then there was the signature of heat by it when it stopped. This is where it used the device we found evidence of. Then it moved off the property. This not a bum, Acacia said. I feel it. They had four of the dragons set up watch and scan the grounds for a week but nothing came of it. One of the nights it was Acacias turn to keep watch and Tamara kept him company, they were positioned on the top of the house at a corner, they had been diligent for hours, expecting to see something, but it was quiet. They began to relax as the night wore on. At the time they were relieved nothing had happened and nothing did that night nor the next.

It happened about eleven thirty on a Thursday, Albert was caring for the children in the room they used as a nursery. He still is not sure what made him suspicious, but he noticed lights coming toward the compound. He began to pay attention to it when the lights didn't take the normal flight path the regular air traffic took. At first he suspected it was a police action but when it dropped down to tree height he knew it had to be a helicopter and he knew something wasn't right. He used his cell phone and alerted William who was on duty that night. William checked with the local tower and found they had nothing scheduled for the area, it was upon the compound by then. Albert had already rounded up some of the dragons and had raided the armory. It was a good thing, because when they had exited the building, men were pouring out of the helicopter and into the woods next to where it had landed. Tamara watched as the dragons took up places around her, guns in hand. She found Acacia, where do you want me to take the children? Get them to ops. How can something like this be happening in America, it's against the law. We can't do anything about it because we can't have the publicity. They seem to be the same way about it. Think about it, if we had a police action or some kind of scrutiny by the law, how long until we were found out to be dragons. Or the fact our identification for some of us is bogus? Well ,what about the sound of gunfire from all of this shooting? Tamara asked. Hopefully it wont come to that he said. If it does we will deal with the police however we must, and he rushed off. There was a rifle shot, and Tamara turned to the window to see what happened. The helicopter was slowly turning in circles, as the pilot tried to gain control of it. It had tried to leave and someone had shot it. They all had radios, and she heard Williams voice come on the radio. Ben shot it, it's going down. Sure enough they watched as it plummeted to the ground, crashing onto it's side. Some of the men in the forest ran out to try to rescue the ones in the bird, but they left them alone after looking them over. They must be dead, Acacia said.

Another shot rang out and Tamara saw a man in the forest fall, clutching his leg. A shot rang out from the forest and a window in the other room crashed. Take the children, Acacia said as he came back into the room, this might be over in a moment or it might not, we shouldn't take any chances. Tamara grabbed cribs and started pushing them toward the elevator. She parked them outside the elevator door and went for more. As she was starting to enter the room Susan came out pushing cribs also. Take those four down she told Tamara, I'll bring others. Tamara nodded her understanding, she was the only one of them two who knew the code to the ops elevator. She loaded them into the elevator and started down. When she came up for more, the rest of them were waiting outside the elevator door. She took them down and went back up to find Acacia. He was still in the same room, a window was open and he had his rifle sticking out of it. Carefully go down to the library, he instructed her. I heard a noise, there may be someone hurt just outside the big window. She made it down to the library, staying low she opened a window and whispered, anyone there? It's Alexander, came the reply. Anyone hurt? Acacia sent me to ask. No just concrete chips in my eye, got them out no problem. Ok, said Tamara, you need anything? Not now, came the reply. Just then there was another shot, and then another, and she heard a ricochet. I think we wounded another one of them, came Alexander's voice. Looks like they are leaving, he added after a moment.

After half an hour when there no movement out side, and the satellite showing nothing also, they ventured over to the helicopter after looking it over through binoculars. There were two men in the helicopter, one was almost cut in half, and the other had a piece of metal poking through his chest. Tamara had been waiting in the nursery for Acacia and it was him who had informed her about all of this. They lost two men, he was sad she could tell, it was their decision she reminded him. We wounded two, they were down to six men that's why they left. He was worried, she could see it, she tried to comfort him. William told me that they usually stop after loosing five men. That's correct in normal times, but they know we will be twenty four this time, if they know that and what it means, it is possible they may not so easily give up this time. You need to be sure to not worry, she told him, you did good, Alexander has a few scratches, no one else was hurt. Ben and Susan came in. We came to pick up Cameron, she said, Ben picked his son up and hugged him to him. Susan watched them, love and happiness in her eyes. Good to see you both enjoying the baby, Tamara said. She hadn't seen all three of them together before, they made a good family. You have a really good looking kid there Ben, she told him, gently kissing the babies cheek. He beamed, thanks, it's so much better sharing this with some one you love, he was looking at Susan. Did you know Ben was one of them who wounded one of those guys out there? Susan asked Tamara, pride showing in her eyes. Yes, Tamara responded. Susan slapped his thick arm, he's going to make a good father to our little boy, she beamed at him. They put Cameron back in the crib and rolled it out of the room. Acacia and Tamara watched them, he shook his head, who would have known, makes me wonder how many of the women we let go, that might have wanted to stay. Water under the bridge, Tamara said, the timing this time with you two was right all the way around. He nodded agreement.

Chapter Seven

Peter and Alexander showed up a few days later, a blond in the SUV with them. Peter introduced each of them to her, not explaining who they were, he just called them friends and coworkers. The girls name was Samantha, she stayed with them a few days then left, spending most of her time with Peter. When Tamara asked Alexander what happened he just shrugged, she liked Peter better. When she left Peter came to Acacia and reported, Tamara was there as well. She was a little uncomfortable with this many people around and no good explanation, he told them. She was on vacation from work and needed to return, she is a nurse. She wants to come and visit again in a few months, I believe she was serious. You like her? Acacia asked. To soon to tell for me, as for her she didn't let me know anything. She is shy and really sweet, I know that for sure.

Everyone was constantly watching and alert, you could see it in their actions. Weeks went by and then a month, all stayed calm. Tamara! Acacia was calling her. Yes, she responded, here at the bed folding the boy's clothes. He walked smiling into the room. She was happy to see him smile, he had been a little to solemn for her liking since the attack. The boys and I are going to dig a hole in the trees to bury the helicopter in. They had buried the two men that same night after trying to get finger prints from them to no avail. They are bored, would you and Susan take care of the children? Sure, she smiled at his enthusiasm. They're not used to having this much spare time, he said as if to explain it to himself. They want to have another pool party if that's ok with you, he asked her. It's ok with me, why are they asking me? They want you and Susan to come, they said if you didn't want it now they would wait. When do they want to party? Tonight, he said nibbling her ear. Let's do it, Tamara slapped her hands together in excitement, I'll call the caterers.

They had sat up music and lights, and the pool was warm. The food was really good, the caterers had out done themselves. She watched as these men of more then an hundred years old, laughed and played like ten year old boys. The laughter was coming from all around, and cries of fun and mirth filled the air. She was relaxed, laying on a lounge beside Acacia, a drink in her hand. He was watching the area around the house, peering out into the woods from time to time. Periodically he would laugh at some antic one of the dragons would pull. The children were in cribs inside the library again, but they would soon outgrow them, already the dragons had pulled the playpens out of storage. Tamara looked into the sky, it was dark and the stars were thick. I was a beautiful if cold night, she would have to get back in the water in a few minuets to warm up. Acacia wouldn't even feel the cold for a good time longer, that tough dragon skin was not a myth.

As she slipped back into the pool she saw movement in the woods, and she froze. It moved again. She was out in a flash yelling at all of them they had company. A dragon can move fast when it has to, and the boys were out of the pool and rushing into the house taking up weapons by the time she was able to get inside. They dashed by her to take up their places as she rushed through the doors. Susan was right behind her, they rushed the cribs to the inner wall of the hall placing three walls between them and the outside. There were shots fired from the woods, the flash of the guns muzzles bright in the darkness. There was a shot from the house and Tamara saw someone in the woods, run back into the darkness, deeper into the woods. Another shot and someone in the woods cried out. There was a shot from the woods, and she heard a dragon near by swear. Forest! You ok? The worried voice of Roman asked. Yea, just grazed my arm. Get inside, another voice commanded, Have one of the girls look at it. It can wait, he responded. There was silence again. Another shot from the house, got one, A voice said, she couldn't tell who. Who is watching the other side of the house? Tamara asked Susan. I saw Ben and Albert heading that way, I don't know who else. I'm going to go over there and check on them. Susan nodded her acknowledgement.

Tamara crept over to the other side of the house, keeping clear of the windows. She found William, watching through an open window with binoculars. That's the second time we caught them before they were ready, I hope our luck holds true. How did they get past the perimeter security? She asked. That's what I was asking myself, William said, there should have been no way. What about by parachute? She asked. If they could land with that precision maybe. That would be hard to do, but I can not come up with another explanation. Their leaving, Leslie had walked up to them, we're going to let the dogs loose. Peter came rushing in, Albert has been shot in the chest. William and Leslie ran after Peter as he ran back out of the room. Get the children into the nursery, he told Tamara they may return, I'll call you with a report on Albert, he said , seeing the concern in her eyes. Acacia ran out of the room.

The dragons already had moved Albert to the infirmary. He was moving around so we thought it would be ok to move him, they responded to Leslie's angry question as to why they moved a wounded man. He bent to examine Albert on the examination bed, he rubbed his back and pulled his hand out with blood on it. It went clean through so I will not have to operate he said to Albert. I am having trouble breathing, Albert whispered. The bleeding is minimal, it went through your lung but I don't believe it severed any large blood vessels, I'll monitor you for a while, if it goes as I think you will be up in a few days. It is very painful, Albert whispered. I'll give you something for that, now rest, I'll be here when you wake. Leslie turned to Acacia, the bullet went clean through, must have been a standard bullet not a soft one. He doesn't seem to be bleeding much internally, I will keep an eye on him if anything changes I'll call you. He should be fine in a few days.

I'm going to get dressed, William said. Not a bad idea, Acacia agreed, and went to find Tamara. The children had all been crying when they had finally got them to the nursery, Susan and Tamar had managed to comfort them, Susan while holding Cameron. Tamara was rocking some of them and they were a familiar place, they all soon were back asleep. Tamara went to the bedroom and dressed. Acacia came in after a few minuets, he dressed and after kissing her on the cheek said, I'll be in ops. The dogs all came in, and the dragons dressed all in black went out to investigate. After about an hour they came back in. We got another one, probably dead. Good Susan interrupted, we never did anything to those sons of bitches. There is a whole lot of blood out there, William went on, I doubt he made it to a hospital in time. They probably have a medic with them, Acacia said. Doubt it mattered, William said. Will it make them stop, is the question, Alexander said. We need to be more careful, Acacia warned, we're making a lot of assumptions about a lot of things. They all agreed.

They celebrated Christmas and then New Year, all very quietly. Albert had healed quickly, Leslie had said the damage had been minimal for the area he had been hit, he had been lucky. Spring came, and the time change, and they still lay low. One day Tamara suggested to Acacia that they all move to a different location. This is the safest place we have, he assured her, we spent ten years getting it ready. I know it seems difficult, Acacia said, but we have another ten to eleven years of this, it really depends on a large number of variables. Well I wouldn't change a thing then, she said, as long as your with me. Have you ever tried to find out who these people are and stop them before they come after you? You know, like a preemptive strike? She asked. We investigated them one time, but they live off the grid, even those two from the helicopter that you saw, they didn't have finger prints, they had burned them off before coming here. Well, they seem to be keeping track of you, she told him, so that means they're getting information from somewhere. That means someone is getting them information, you should be able to find that person, right? He thought about it for a while, I do know someone, I'll call them tomorrow. As a matter of fact, he went on, I believe I know someone who will know someone who will know, or be able to find out for us.

They stayed up late going over all the information they could find from the last few attacks looking for the common denominator, they were all exhausted and slept late the next day. Only two of the dragons stayed up and kept watch. Tamara awoke to Acacia trying to sneak out of bed, there was just a glimmer of light outside from the rising sun. Where you going? Get back here, I want you. He slipped back into bed nuzzling her, his face between her breasts. Thirty minuets later, the sun was into the sky, they showered. Where did you learn all your moves in bed? After nine hundred years, you learn a lot about many things. He stepped out of the shower, but she wanted to stay a while longer. I'll be in ops, he said, I'm going to follow up on what we did last night. I'll be there as soon as I take care of Annabelle.

Tamara felt sexy so she fixed herself up like she was going out. Annabelle was laying in her crib playing. She picked her up and gave her a bottle for a while, then finished off feeding her with some baby food until she refused any more. Down in ops, she watched Acacia scrolling through data on the computer. She loved to watch him when he was focused, she thought the look on his face was sexy. He spotted her, glancing up for a moment. Motioning for her to look at the screen, he said excitedly, take a look at this. Look here, see here where this company has made numerous inquires about us as a company. At first it would look like they were interested in hiring us. But look at this, look at the questions, they're aimed toward us as a group, not as a company. A friend of mine sent this to me a few minuets ago, so I haven't had a chance to spend much time on it. Now if you search this company that is inquiring, look at this, they have a little offshoot company here, see these records, he said, pointing at some financial data. No, not really she said, but proceed. He smiled at that, look at the money, it comes from here and goes there. This little company is really pulling the strings. What does the little company do? she asked. It's a paramilitary school, a perfect cover. They would train the customers during the day, and use the facilities for their own training in the night and maybe weekends. I'm going to make a few phone calls, give me a little time and I'll know a lot more. He moved his chair over to a phone near by and dialed. She studied the figures and noticed that a good deal of money was going into another company. Into a resort that she had heard of, a resort in the mountains not to far from them now. Acacia rolled the chair back to the computer and started to pull up a screen. Acacia look at this, she said pointing. He looked at the screen as she pointed to what she had found, here and here. Oh, he said, this would be where they stay and train. He paused, I have an idea, he said, and spent a few minuets to give her an idea of his plans. You be careful, Acacia, You promise? Yes, he said distracted, but he was grinning from ear to ear.

Two nights later, she was standing and watching ten of the dragons put the last of some items into the back of one of the Hummers. William, Peter, Roman and Forest, stripped down and placed their clothes into the back of the Hummer on the other items and closed the hatch. They changed, and were airborne. She watched them until they were out of sight. Acacia was standing beside her, he kissed her on the cheek and hugged her. Don't worry, he said, the plan is good, and it's simple, not much to go wrong. She wanted to take him and hug him and keep him safe, but she knew he was his own man, and anyway nothing is safe in life. She loved him for who he was and this was a dragon with responsibilities to others, responsibilities he had made prior to his commitment to her. She would support him, and love him, that's all she could do. He walked around to the front door of the Hummer, she gave him one last hug. You keep me in the know, she pointed her finger at him, you have a radio for that. He waved at her.

She went to the com in ops and listened to the chatter, sporadic as it was. After two hours it heated up. William came on the radio, he was breathing hard. We have the right place, there is a large building, well fortified. There were still some of the guys out. We picked one of they up, you should have seen Ben, snagged him while flying, I never seen a dragon fly like he did, he must love the woman of his, he's went deep into protective mode. Knocked the guy out, so he didn't get to kill himself, we checked him and he didn't have any identification or finger prints, just like the others. When he wakes up we should be able to get a lot of information from him. We have him tied up in the Hummer. Did you check his teeth? Acacia asked. Yes, nothing. Check his arms close to the wrist. I'm checking. Found it, how did you know? I found it on the others, something new they came up with. What do you think they tell theses guys about us that make them willing to kill themselves? I have no idea but be sure to tie his hands to his sides. Right. You almost here? William asked? Ten minuets, we'll be there. Good, it's cold up here and I want to get some clothes on. It's not cold here, Acacia said. Smart ass, William said and signed off. You get all of that sweet? Acacia asked. Yea, thanks, Tamara responded. She listened as they chatted back and forth, as they did their worked. She could see them in her minds eye, as they poured gas from the containers at places all around compound.

Call in when your ready, Acacia asked them. After a few moments voices began to call out, one is ready, six is ready, three is ready, four is ready, five is ready, two is ready. Ok ignite, get back here and get dressed. She listened and waited after about five minuets Acacia came on the radio, coming home, it's going to get hot around here.

They were supposed to drive a few miles from the sight, stop and Acacia was going to do a flyover to check what happened. The radio came alive again, there goes the fire trucks, then after a short time, we're stopping. I'm going to go check. Tamara felt herself tense, this was the part of the plan that was the most risky. Acacia was going to fly back over the compound so they would know how bad they had hurt them. It was important they know, but the fires would be in full burn by then, he could be seen. He also had to be careful of the updrafts caused from the fires. She waited for what seemed an hour, then William came on the radio, he's back Tamara. Thanks, William. After a few minuets Acacia came on. Tamara, it looks good, the fire surrounded them so they couldn't leave, it caused a good deal of damage to the outside, and they will have to deal with the authorities, tomorrow we will place a call of someone being murdered, it will show it came from this area. They will have to deal with the authorities about that also. That will tie them up for enough time to get another plan ready. It looked as if no one was harmed, as you asked. Good, she said, thanks. We will be back in a few hours, Brock will stay and make the call, then fly back. See you when you get here, she signed off.

They took the man they captured to a remote sight in the same mountains, they tried everything short of torture to get him to talk, including slapping him around pretty good. They decided in the end to let him go with a message to the others that they were coming after them. Disappointed they started home.

Chapter Eight

The next day she was discussing a new plan with him something she had thought of but didn't know if he could work it. We could try a hostile take over, they are open to it, and it would cause them grief. But it wouldn't be the parent company, you understand? But we would be in the inside if we accomplished it, she countered, and if not it would keep them busy. Also at the same time we could harass them with little problems, fire at the office building, shipments being hijacked, things like that. You and the dragons would be good at such things. If we keep them jumping, they wouldn't have time for pursuing us. We're tied up here if we don't, and I think the boys would rather be occupied, ask them, Tamara suggested.

She had been right, the dragons were itching to do something. Acacia put them each to a task, after explaining to them the whole plan. They gathered all their money together, putting it in escrow. Tapped their lines of credit, in case something went wrong. Located the buildings belonging to those companies and bought the supplies they needed. They were ready. They had a finale meeting, rehearsed the plan and checked each of their parts. In three days, they would start. The lawyers had started already. The next day the lawyers called to tell Acacia that the plan was working and the reporters were calling and he need some direction as to their response. They also reported that the other side, having been caught unaware, were scrambling to counter the offers. That should tie them up for a while, William sounded excited. The plan for the first building was to set off the fire sprinklers and make a mess. They had placed a large piece of iron on an adjoining roof. Alexander was to fly, and pick it up, and break out a window on the third floor. And get out fast. As soon as the window is broken, Brock and Peter would access the building through the window and set off the sprinklers by means of a small fire. Flying in and out. The same thing would be done on the fourth floor by Timothy, Roman and Forest, only on the opposite side of the building. They figured it would take at least a week for the office's affected to get back up and running.

The night came for the plan to be executed, and it went off without a hitch. Two days and they would do another building in a city a days drive away. Tamara manned the radios, she liked it because she felt like she was part of the action and she could keep an eye on Annabelle, who was now crawling. They had kept tabs on the job in the mountains and found that their work had seemed to shut down the place for over two weeks. Crews had been seen working on the outside for that long.

The next building proved a good deal harder. The glass didn't break on one side but only cracked. Peter flew through the cracked window to finish breaking it. The second problem arose when the device they had made to start the fire fizzled. They set off the sprinklers another way but it put them behind schedule and that made them all concerned.

The next project was a hijacking of some delicate machines that were needed at one of their facilities so that an important project might not be completed by a deadline. They had two of them fly and land on the trailer of the Simi that was making the delivery of the machines. They dropped a weighted tarp over the windows obscuring the vision of the driver. When the crew stopped the truck to remove it, Ben and Alexander evicted them from the truck and drove it away, taking their phones as well, leaving them stranded on a remote country road. They drove the truck to a prearranged place where they hid it, it would be found in a few days or maybe a week. It went well except the tarp was much more difficult to get into place then they had anticipated. They would have to work that out if they did this again.

Next they did a few low tech things, they called a gas leak scare on one of the corporate office buildings. Then they took out the phone and power line that fed the neighborhood where a CEO of importance lived and blocked the only road out with a few trees. Easy work for dragons. Then they rested and waited.

Acacia and Tamara were watching Annabelle as she struggled to keep her balance. She tottered and then took her first step. It was late August and it was very warm out. They were setting out under a tree not far from the pool. Their labors in sabotage had as it turned out were most successful. They had flown surveillance where they could, with that and the news, they found that they had caused a good deal of disruption and chaos, so they waited. Roman came walking toward them from the house Acacia arose and turned to help Tamara with Annabelle when a gun shot echoed off the walls of the house. Roman's left side spun backward and he fell to the ground. Telling her to protect Annabelle, Acacia was out of his clothing in record time and changed. With a great leap and the ripple of sinew and muscle he was airborne and off toward the woods, Tamara calling after him to be careful. Call Leslie, were his last words before changing. Placing Annabelle against the tree, she shielded her with her own body and phoned Leslie. She turned and watched as Acacia dove into the woods, it was apparent that he had found a prey. He reminded her of a falcon as his wings twisted as he took aim at his moving target, then he was shooting downward.

Making a split second decision she grabbed Annabelle and made a dash for the house. She passed Leslie and Ben coming out and yelled, "Roman's been shot." She watched from the window as Ben and Leslie after checking Roman's wounds, carried him toward the house. Forest came up to her, panting from exertion. What happened? Someone in the forest shot Roman. Forest's face grew pale. How bad? I'm not sure, she took his hand, Forest, I'm sure it will be alright. You love him greatly? He stared at her, you know? Is it obvious? He asked. Yes, to me it is, she told him, you should go to him, he will want you to be there. They brought Roman through the door way. Forest went over to them, can I do anything to help? He asked, as they lay him on the couch. Yes, Leslie said, warm water and cloths, until I see how bad it is, I don't want to move him again. He ripped his shirt back revealing a wound just over his left nipple blood oozing from it with each breath. Leslie checked Roman's pulse again, it missed his heart, pulse is still strong. Could you get me a gurney from the infirmary, he told Tamara, when she asked them if she could help. He prompted her when she paused for a moment, Go on, he'll be just fine.

Relief rushed over her and she hurried to get the gurney. She passed Forest on her way, He is going to be fine, Leslie told me just now. She watched his face relax in relief. Thanks, he said, hurrying away with towels and water from the kitchen. She entered the room with the gurney, just as Acacia came through a different doorway. Is everyone ok, he asked. William came in the door just behind him, yes, we're all ok, just Roman was hurt, William told him. There was no other intruder, I checked the grounds with the satellite. It was the same one we captured the other day, Acacia told them, I would assume they sent him here as a punishment, thinking he would die and maybe take one of us with him. He could have volunteered, Forest suggested, something like redemption. Well, he will bother us no more, I ripped him in two with my talons, Acacia said with relish, we will bury both parts as soon as we have seen to Roman. He turned to Leslie, how is he? He will be ok? Acacia's eyes were swimming with tears. Yes, Leslie said, a minor operation to remove the bullet and repair his lung. Acacia's stern face softened, go then, take good care of him, can I do anything to help? No, I need time and Ben to help. Roman's eyes came open, he struggled for a moment until he oriented himself. Don't struggle, Leslie comforted him, a minor operation and you will be all right. Roman smiled weakly.

Chapter Nine

Tamara went to take Roman his lunch, she had brought it to him the last two days. It had been five days since he had been shot and he was doing really well. Forest and Timothy had left the day before to negotiate some purchases for the business, so she had volunteered to bring up his meals. Why did you decide to stay with us? He asked her out of a clear blue sky. She looked intently at him, I fell in love with Acacia the moment I saw him standing there naked and unashamed, stupid I know, but I was enthralled, that's all there is to it. Dragons do that to people sometimes. He looked deep into her eyes, you love him deeply, don't you? You know, she said, changing the subject. I see the same look in Forest eyes when he talks about you as I see in Ben's eye when he talks about Susan. His face reddened, yes, I suppose you do. She took the dishes and turned to leave. You know a female dragon is more then we ever expected, we thought it was never to be again. Forest is going to look for a mate while he's away, it will be hard on me but I hope he finds someone like you. She turned back, You know it will never change the way he feels about you. He nodded, I know, come see me tomorrow, Leslie said I could get up tomorrow. I'll be here Roman, count on it.

The next day William was talking to Timothy on the phone, it was a protocol for anyone to call twice a day if away from the others, when he heard him yell out and the phone went dead. William began to monitor the emergency channels when ever their seemed to be a problem it was also protocol. It was a good thing that they did. When William lost the call from Timothy he turned on the emergency channel and heard the call that went out calling an ambulance to an accident on the road that Timothy had been traveling on. Within ten minuets there were dragons in the air and some on the ground in their own medical response van headed for the accident site. They were hoping to get there before the paramedics did as they couldn't have a dragon being examined by any trained medical worker. Tamara was manning the com again and listened as Leslie and Ben in the van communicated with Alexander and Brock in a Hummer following behind them. Acacia and William should be there any minuet, Brock said, they flew over us about five minuets ago, it's a good thing this didn't happen very far away from the compound. After a moment William's voice came over the radio, there is already two ambulances here and one is just driving away with Forest, and the second is loading Timothy in as we speak. The good thing is they don't seem to be hurt so bad we couldn't care for them at the compound. Getting them away from these guys will be difficult though.

Ben came on the line, you should try to bribe them into letting you take him. There should be two thousand dollars in the emergency pouch you took with you. Good idea, Acacia said, I'll do that right now. William came on the line, he's getting the money, we'll let you know how it goes as soon as we can.

Alexander came on the line reporting they would be at the scene in about two minuets with the van. Tamara waited, leaning over the com panel tense as she waited to hear what happened. It was only a moment then Brock came on the radio to report that it looked like Acacia was going to be successful in getting them to release Timothy, now they would have to worry about getting Forest away before he arrived at the hospital. Tamara turned the volume up on the emergency channel. You guys had better hurry she said after listening for a short time, they just reported their ETA as ten minuets, they also reported Forest as stable, with a broken leg and some possible internal bleeding and a good amount of minor abrasions. We can handle that no problem, Leslie said over the radio, but how are we going to get him away from the paramedics? Acacia came back on the line, I'm going to fly to the other ambulance and stop it, I need the van to follow me as soon as possible.

How are you going to stop the ambulance, Brock asked? I'm not sure but William and I will think of something, you just get that van to where we are. Ok, Brock said we'll be there. How is Timothy, asked Acacia? Just bruised up, he'll be just fine, Leslie said, Forest was driving and that was the side they were hit on. What about the driver of the other car, is he ok, asked Tamara? Yes, said Leslie, it was a delivery van and he it just slightly bruised. Some one needs to stay there and claim they were the driver, Tamara said, or the police will follow up and find us by the registration. That might work, said Brock, I'll stay. See if you can get the other party to leave in the ambulance, Acacia added, that way the cops have to interview him some where else so he can't contradict you. I'll do what I can, Brock said.

Acacia flew to the ambulance, he grabbed the side of it with his claws and flapping his wings pushed it to the side of the road. The driver fought it but after trying for a short time he finally pulled over to the side of the road to take a look at the vehicle. William landed a short ways away and quickly dressed. He took a gun from the emergency bag and raced over to the ambulance as

Leslie and Ben pulled up behind them. Acacia came walking up at the same time as the driver came around the side of the van. Just wait right there, William said, we are not going to hurt you we are just taking your passenger with us. The mans hands went up, that man needs medical attention. I will be taking him for care, he is a friend of ours, Acacia said, we don't want any trouble just let us take him ok? The other paramedic came out of the double doors at the back of the van, you might as well let them take him, he said, I haven't been able to get a needle into him anyway, they all keep breaking.

You people the driver stuttered, will be able to help him? Yes, Acacia answered, we have the facilities. What about our financial loss for this call, our boss will need paid. William took out some money, here would five hundred dollars work, he asked? Yes, that would be enough, the man answered, but you will not get any receipt this will have to be off the books since we had already started the run. That's not a problem with us, Acacia said, we just are the only ones able to help our partner there, Acacia said, tilting his head toward the van. They exchanged money and they moved Forest into the van. This never happened, the man said, you people are from the government I assume? Some thing like that, Acacia said, getting into the van, and thanks from us and our friend. Yea, take care then the man said. What are you going to tell the hospital? Asked Acacia. He insisted to get out, that is all we can say, the driver said.

I thought we could trust him Acacia said, he seemed trustworthy alright, William agreed. They had just watched a news cast where the two paramedics had told how that Forest had walked away from them in exact detail. The only thing they left out was the part about them breaking needles trying to get them into Forest. Let's keep an eye on that for awhile, Acacia said, see what happens with it. If later we need to do something more we can do it then.

Acacia was in ops, he and William were working on the plans for another strike on their enemies. Acacia seemed to be worried, he hadn't really been himself. The night before his lovemaking had been what she would term frantic. She looked over William's shoulder as he pointed at a place on an aerial view map. The map was of a distribution center with many large trucks parked. If we stop movement in and out of this one, William said to her inquiries, it will bring most of their production to a halt. We estimate seventy percent of their products get their components through here. We can take out the roadway and the power, and keep them out for at least three days. The only thing is, it will also affect some innocent companies as well. I don't want to do that, but there seems to be no choice. Maybe I can compensate them at another time Acacia said. Why? William asked, we are only doing this for our survival. Acacia brushed back his hair, I know, I know, but it still bothers me.

They walked together toward the elevator, do you think it is over? She asked. He knew what she was talking about. We have taken out quite a few of them, I just don't know if it is enough. There is no way of really knowing, she agreed. Acacia? Yes? How does it feel when you change? He smiled at her, what brought this on? When Roman was shot I began to realize that I know little of your kind. My kind? He teased. When I say kind, I am speaking of a special breed, something of magnificence. He bowed, why thank you madam. Well, he said. It is like a tickle all over your body. Your mind is held in time for a moment, nothing around you seems to happen, your just there. Then all of a sudden there is more light and everything is more defined. You can see well close up and you can see a small bird a mile away. You have use of a tail, you feel it as it rubs the ground and you can move it to hold things and to hit things. You can run like the wind, and you feel the breeze as it rustles your wings. You spread your wings and flap them feeling the power in them. You feel yourself lifting off the ground as you put your whole effort in the motion. The strain of the effort has the feel of having really great sex, and you sometimes stir in that area. You smell the people below you and the animals that are there as well. You here the sounds they make as you pass silently over head. Then you fly gliding toward the ground, just before you get there you bank letting the wind bring you to a complete stop, you change and drop the few feet to the ground. She stood mesmerized, I can never have that, she said, but I would give a lot if I could.

Why do they say that dragons can breath fire? We can, but not to the extent that is widely depicted, I'll show you next time I'm changed. That is how Brock started the fire when the device we made didn't work. It made him have to cycle another change that night, he had to rest a full day to get his strength back. That's incredible, she whispered, when will the children be able to change? As they reach puberty, they will be going about their business and accidentally change. We pay special attention to them at that time in their life, he explained farther, I have thought that it is one of the reasons our people go around naked, we watch the children and keep them in a safe place for the first change, it would be hard to tell if they were reaching puberty if they were dressed all of the time. Also if they were clothed they would ruin the clothes and there is a small chance of the clothing hurting them also. I have never opened you flap again, she said as the thought hit her, will I soon? You can tonight if you wish, he said.

Can dragons mate in dragon form? Yes, we mate in flight. She became excited, you have to tell me all about it! He laughed, now? Yes now! she said. Well it is a beautiful thing. They had come to a door to the outside. Come on, he said, motioning for her to come out side with him. The day was hot, he said, tonight will be a good time for flying, I will take you with me, he caressed her face, looking at her lovingly. There is room for you to ride just above my wings, it is, I'm told, a touch scary but your welcome if you want. Yes, I would like that, Tamara said excitedly.

Susan came out the door carrying Annabelle and Cameron, one under each arm. She placed Annabelle on the ground and pointed out her parents to her. Annabelle came toward them tottering. Her father reached to pick her up as she approached, as he picked her up she said in a breathy voice, "caisa" speaking her first words. We were walking by the window and she wanted to go outside, Susan explained, I saw you both and thought maybe she had seen you also. Susan placed Cameron on the ground, he decided to sit. Did you hear her? Tamara asked Acacia. She tried to say something, Acacia laughed with happiness. Tried! She was calling my name, caisa, Acacia said, excitement filling his eyes. Her first word and it's your name, I'm defeated. Tamara put on an act of great loss. That is defeat, Susan agreed, after all you did for her, and the first word is her fathers name. Why is it surprising that a young lady would notice strength and virility? Acacia asked. Oh is that what it is, all I see is a self centered bastard, Tamara chuckled, and a hunk. Now if she is looking for a hunk, she got it right.

Have you went by to see Roman today? Acacia asked, changing the subject. Yes, this morning. I'm taking him lunch, Tamara said. He is getting out of the infirmary today, I doubt that Leslie will be able to keep him in there if he can walk. No he wont, Acacia agreed, he will wanting to leave. If you ask him to stay another day or so more, it would be a lot easier on Leslie. Your right, he said do you want to go with me to see him? You will ask him then? Of course, Acacia said, I think I can keep him there a little longer. Acacia? the place where he was shot, it is almost gone, it looks as if there will not be even a scare. Dragon skin, he told her, if he hadn't been a dragon, the damage from the bullet would have been much worse. His skin will not even show a trace of the wound in a few more days.

They started toward the house, William came out the door, strode over to them, Forest just arrived, he was successful on all accounts. He found him a girl? Tamara asked excited. A girl it is, and she's seventeen. Oh, Tamara said. She will be eighteen in two months. He is quite taken, William chuckled. It is good for the dragons to be looking for love after it being the way it was for so long, she said. He agreed. What about you, you going to start looking? Tamara asked William. I'm already engaged, he said.

She raised an eyebrow, yes? To taking care of the dragons, when I decide to break that engagement, I will look for another. I admire you William, Tamara said as they walked into the house. I am thankful we are on the same side. Well the girl will be here day after tomorrow, we'll see what happens, William said.

Forest met them as they passed through the hall into the living area. This is Acacia, his wife Tamara, William head of security, and Annabelle, he said, taking her up and kissing her on the cheek. This is Breanne, we met at Risario's, he said a big smile on his face. Nice place, she said, looking around. Thanks, it belongs to the company, Acacia said. Here, let me show you around, Tamara said, taking Breanne by the arm. I have to discuss things with Acacia, Forest said to Breanne, I'll find you in a little bit. We are a little out of the ordinary here, Tamara said to Breanne, there are twelve of the employees staying here but there are only two women. We treat each other like family though. You people don't expect any sharing, right? No, Tamara had to laugh, none of that. Forest is really a gentleman, Breanne said, that's what made me like him, he held the door for me, can you believe that? Yea, some of the guys here seem to have an old fashioned streak. This is the formal living room here, we don't seem to have a need to use it much. This is the dinning area, here and in the library is where we do most of our socializing. Out here is the pool, she took her out a doorway. That is one hell of a pool, Breanne said. Yes, it really is very nice, Tamara agreed.

Why do so many of you live here, it's like a commune? The type of work they do in security makes it much easier if they all reside in the same place, it's not required, but most of them are single with no families to worry with. Single and hot, Annie added. Their not gay, are they? I mean all these hot guys in a house, sounds gay. No, like I said, it's work. Breanne do your parents know where you are? Yea, they met Forest and said I should go and check out his place. When do you graduate? I did in June, I'm going to college in September. What's your major? History. We're going to be eating in about an hour, you want to have lunch with us? Is Forest going to be there? I'm sure he will be, you can meet all the others except one, he was hurt on the last job, he's recovering. What's his name? His name is Roman. Roman, yea, Forest talked about him, Breanne said, sounded like a nice guy. Yes, Tamara agreed, he's real sweet.

All of them except Roman was setting around the table. The boys were on their good behavior, completely dressed and polite, the conversation ran along football, movies and what ever was in the news lately. Breanne was animated, and dearly loved the attention she was getting from the dragons. Every once in a while, Tamara would catch a glance that passed between a few of the dragons. They were not sure what to think of this girl either. Forest excused himself and told Breanne he would be right back. He took a plate of food and left. Breanne asked Tamara, where he was going. He is taking Roman some food, he'll be right back. The dragons took turns politely asking Breanne questions. They found out she came from Southern California, her father had made it in a specialty baking company, not rich, but not hurting either. They were liberal, and she was instructed to keep an open mind and enjoy life. She was out to have a good time.

Forest came back into the room about twenty minuets later, when some of the dragons inquired he said, Breanne is staying in the spare room, I'm taking her back to her parents in the morning. I'll get it ready, Tamara and Susan said together, as they excused their selves. I've got to go over some things with William about an upcoming job, Acacia said, he and William excused themselves. As she left, Tamara heard the other dragons excusing their selves. In the guest room, Tamara and Susan had a good laugh as they changed out the sheets on the bed and freshened up the room. He can't really like her for real, can he? He might, Tamara answered her, it takes all kinds. I just want to see her face when he changes, Susan said, it would be priceless. The door opened and Breanne and Forest came in, they were really laughing hard about something. Tamara and Susan, having finished, left to check on the children. They were all sleeping, Alexander had checked on them periodically while they were all having lunch and now it was Tamara's time to watch them. She woke them all up and just turned them all loose on the carpet and started on a new book. Susan came in after about an hour, she took Cameron and thanked her for watching him. He was a good size boy, it looked like he was going to be the biggest, thick and broad like his father.

She put down her book after a while and went around checking diapers. Changed a few and settled back to her book. About ten o'clock. Timothy and Acacia came in. Timothy was going to watch the children, She and Acacia was going to bed. She picked up Annabelle. You had bettered do a diaper check, she cautioned Timothy, I lost track of time, sorry. Good book? he asked. Yea, and I'm getting to a really good part. Acacia picked up Annabelle, see you in the morning Timothy. See you, he answered absently. What do you think of Breanne? Acacia asked her as they walked toward their room. She placed a struggling Annabelle on the carpet. She is a immature girl but she and Forest really seemed to hit it off. I say we give it time and see where it goes. That's what William thought. I'm not ready for bed, let's go see a movie, make it like a date. Sure she answered eagerly. Let's go shower first, Acacia said, I feel rancid. After a quick shower, they went to the theater.

Chapter Ten

Later that night they left Annabelle with Timothy, and went to the roof. Tamara watch in anticipation as Acacia stripped and changed. His head came around and he nibbled her neck, his dragon whiskers tickling her cheek. She caressed his head, rubbing behind his ears. You gorgeous hunk, do you know how much I love you. It doesn't matter which form your in. She saw for the first time he had nipples in this form. She reached and pinched them lightly, then caressed them with her hands. She rubbed down his belly where the soft scales were, her hands running over the cleft of his flap. His tail came around and rubbed between her legs, finding just the right spot. She knew he had done this before. Her hand reached into his pouch and clutched him, he was still limp and she felt around checking what she found, imagining more in her mind. He nuzzled her ear and she moved from under him. He lowered his head she straddled his neck and slid down into a comfortable position just above his wings. He stretched his wings to their full and with a leap they were airborne. She cried out half in exhilaration half in fright and then settled in for the ride. His powerful wings moved them quickly upward, she looked toward the ground, the buildings were like toys. He still climbed higher it was getting cold, he leveled out and began to circle, spiraling slowly toward the ground. He brought his head back to look at her, she kissed him on his muzzle. Before long he was landing on the roof, he changed. he was standing there before her breathing hard. When we mate in dragon form, we go a little higher up then I took you. We free fall, the male on top then he wraps his tail around hers. Clutching her in his arms, they both glide down, they have sex as they go. She looked at his naked body and reached down fondling him, she whispered in his ear, take me now.

The dragons were loading the Hummer, they slid long iron bars in under the seat. They were going to drop them on the power lines, shorting them out. There were cordless chain saws, to take out trees to block the road. Tamara was worried, she always did worry, but she knew how dedicated they all were to keeping all of the dragons safe. She had done everything she could and now she took her place at the com, she was going to stay there all the times they would be exposed to any danger, it would give her peace of mind. Roman came out to watch he would not be going this trip but would be in ops. He had wanted to go and had argued that point with William, but out of respect to Acacia's request he stayed. Leslie came in an hour later, bringing her lunch. Thanks for your help with Roman, he is healing very well, but resting and not off running around will make him heal faster and better. You know, he said, I'm over three hundred years old. A hundred years older then Roman. We all have seen so much. I came to work in America right after the civil war. I immigrated from Belgium. I found Acacia by accident one night, we both were flying over the same patch of woods looking for deer. He noticed the questioning look on her face and explained farther. I was staying with a family, helping them by doing work on a ranch for room and board. The owner had gotten hurt and I was getting food for the family. It is easy for a dragon to bring down a deer, much easier then trying to shoot one. Acacia was working with some surveyors, he was scouting forward for them, he also was needing food for them and was going to bring a deer back to camp. We met and talked, he came with me to the farm. We both worked until the owner was back on his feet and then we moved west, following the push of the settlers. Where is Acacia from? She asked, I've never thought to ask him. He is from Italy, he was a map maker for the government before immigrating to America. We all have had many occupations over time, we can not stay in one place for more then about seven years, people begin to ask questions.

Has Acacia spoken to you about finding a new place? No, not yet, she answered. I'm not surprised since we just started talking over that subject over ourselves late yesterday, Leslie told her. William is of the mind that we should move to another country, I'm not to sure of that. We have all been in America for a long time. What country was he thinking of? She asked him. I don't know, he didn't say but he was saying he is concerned of the government keeping to close a tab on people, it's not to bad now, but it will soon be much worse. When is the seven years up at this location? She asked him. One year and a month, but we do have a little leeway, there is much we need to do. We expect to get started as soon as the others get back from the project their on now? We want you to go and look for property with us. We? She asked him. All of us, he looked at her, Tamara, we all will be involved in this, but you, me, and Acacia, will be doing the leg work if you would like to help us. That would be my pleasure, she assured him.

The com became active as the dragons had reached their destination, they parked a few miles away from the site. The warehouses backed up to a small hill and a roadway passed in front of them, they would target the power line running into the area, dropping the iron bars onto the lines shorting them out, then drop some trees onto the roadways leading out, they only had to wait until dusk. She listened to the chatter on the com, as they talked, preparing for the nights job. After an hour or so, the chatter settled down and the waiting started. She admired the professional efficiency that they operated with. Orders were followed without back talk, the talk was only about the task at hand. After about an hour and a half, Acacia came on the com and started going back over the plan. A half an hour later, they shorted out the first of the power lines. Moving farther away from the warehouse, they took out an even larger power line. They accessed the water mains in the streets and shut down a city block around the warehouse. Albert reported sprinkler alarms going off all around. We have about ten minuets men before the officials get here. Acacia warned. East road is blocked, Brock said. About two minuets later, Ben reported that the west road was blocked. Change and get out, Acacia warned, we have about a minuet. Five minuets later Acacia reported them all having reported in. We're going to go to the hotel, he told Tamara. Call me on the cell, if you would, she asked him, I have something I need to talk to you about. Just give us about thirty minuets. I'll call you, he said.

He called, and on the third ring, she answered. Hey sweet cheeks, he said. Acacia, she said without preamble, I want to live on a mountain. Acacia chuckled, me too. She stopped short on her next preplanned statement, good what country? She queried him. America, he said. Yea, she agreed. In California, he said. Yes, she agreed. But it isn't up to us is it? He said. No, not completely, she agreed. Well think about it and when we get back we will all have a meeting and settle it. She changed the subject, are you going to have to stay another day? Not sure yet, Alexander is going to do a fly over in about an hour, we should know more then. You sure no one saw any of you? Alexander was flying the area, he didn't see or smell anyone. Good, I don't want anything to happen to my babies father. You have given me more reasons to be careful then I have ever had before, Acacia told her, I am only doing what it takes here to get this done properly and nothing else. I know, Tamara said, I'm just looking at everything to deeply, if I can help, I want to. I care about the dragons very deeply and I want to have a hand in establishing this dynasty. It is a terrible thing that people as beautiful, loving and caring as you should be destroyed because of something your ancestors did! It's not right! I know, Acacia sighed, I'm doing all I can. I am as well, Tamara said, I guess I'm not as good at handling the stress as you all. No, you are really doing great, you just don't know it so I'm telling you. Tamara took a deep breath, thanks, I guess I didn't realize how it was getting to me. As soon as you get back, I would like to go look at property, she told him, it sounds like a good deal of fun. I'll take you, we'll get a list and I'll personally fly you. We'll book some motels and I'll fly you to them. Can you do it? I can, we'll make it a special trip just you and me. Your making me hot just thinking about it. I'll call you after an hour and get a report from you, she said. Call me anytime baby.

Tamara dialed the phone, she had Annabelle in her arms. She was beginning to understand that Annabelle knew when her father was gone. She refused to sleep. Hey baby, Acacia answered the phone. What did Alexander find? It looks like it will be a part of one more day before they get this cleaned up, he overheard a worker talking to his partner about it. We'll be back tomorrow morning if nothing changes. Annabelle wont sleep when your away, Tamara told him. She is setting here with me, you want to tell her hi? Sure put her on. She watched as Annabelle and her father played on the phone, Tamara didn't really have any parenting experience, no real examples except her father, he had done ok she thought. The dragons had raised quite a few children, some of them were working around and with her every day, she had watched them to explore how they handled the children. They didn't seem to worry about it, they just did what needed to be done at the time. They always showed their love for the children with hugs, caresses, nibbles on their cheeks and attention when they needed it and not when they wanted. She must be over thinking it. She was going to follow their example and quite worrying. Annabelle threw the phone, Tamara picked it up, I think she's finished talking, we'll let you get some sleep, Acacia told her when she retrieved the phone. Yea, good night, She said. He kissed her through the phone. Good night.

Chapter Eleven

Acacia was standing before her, ready to change, Tamara had a fully packed knapsack on her back, and three destinations. They had booked two motels, and Acacia had assured her he was well able to get her where they were going. He changed and he brought his mouth around to her face and nibbled her cheek. You're a bad boy, she shook her finger at him, you always have only one thing on your mind. She heard a rumble from deep in his chest. Do that again, he did it again. She laughed and hugged his neck down close to his head. You big, beautiful, brute, I love you. He rumbled again, then lowered his head and she found her place on his back. They had an hour of flying then a night at the hotel, a night she was looking forward to. They would rent a car, go see the property in that area, after dark they would fly to the next site and stay at a motel again. Each flight was about an hour, all of them were in the mountains. They had had a meeting the day after the dragons had gotten back from the job. Tamara had set in, but hadn't said much. The meeting had been simple, the suggestion of moving out of the country had only two supporters. When Acacia said that he wanted a mountain place for the ease of defense, the others found that to be the best idea and it was settled quickly. Tamara was just pleased that everyone seemed satisfied with the decision, she didn't want division among them now, especially over her or her ideas. Acacia had flown high, and she was happy he had insisted she dress warm, as she pulled her coat tighter to herself. She had felt the muscles in his neck strain as the had worked to gain altitude, now he was gliding, the air streaming by them in a loud whistle. He started downward, she hugged his neck tighter and kissed the cold scales on the back of his neck. He brought his head around and nudged her in the side in response. They landed in a small clearing not far from the road and she slid off. He changed and relieved himself, pissing on a tree. She handed him his clothes and in a few minuets they were walking up the incline to a resort nestled in the pines and a warm room.

They walked up to the front desk and signed in to their room. Acacia had the man order them a rental for in the morning. They went to their room and showered and made wild love. They were up before seven but she felt rested and ready for the day. They took breakfast at the resorts restaurant and were on the road in short order. The property they went to see was nestled in a small valley, ringed by small peaks with only the road they came in on as access. How far to the nearest town? As dragons fly, ten minuets, by road forty five, maybe a little less he calculated. We have a building about an hour from here, it could be easily be converted to our base of operations. Travel should about the same also, this would make a good site. Tamara pulled some papers from her pack, one hundred acres, she looked around, that would be this whole valley I would guess. There is a seasonal creek that runs, she looked around, from over there where the trees are tall

I would suppose, it says it runs nine months in a normal season. Acacia, are we needing to get off the grid completely? No, not yet, it would be good, but not necessary. We could at this location, she stated flatly. Yes we could. he agreed. I should have brought a picnic lunch, I think the creek is dry now though, we could have ate lunch over on that rock. I don't think this place is right though. They took pictures and drove back to the resort had lunch at a little deli and coffee place and then walked the streets browsing the stores. You never talk about your past, Tamara said to him. You sweet girl, he leaned over and nibbled her neck, since you have come in my life I haven't even thought of the past much. She smiled at him, your slick, but your not going to get off that easy.

Ok, he said, caressing her face with both hands. She felt the rough dragon skin against her face. I will answer all your questions at the room when we go back. Leslie said you came to America right after the civil war. That is right, I didn't know of any other dragons in Europe, or any other place around where more of our people had lived at one time. Did you live among any dragons in Europe? No, I was alone, I do not know if any other dragons exist more then us. What about women? She asked. He chuckled and steered her into a little park that was in a triangle between two roads. Oh, I suppose we could talk about that now. They sat across from each other on a park benches, a table between them. I hope you don't get offended at the history of my life, he said, I suppose that you are most interested in the women I was involved with, most of them were a passing entertainment. It is funny but you would think that I would have been lucky in love having lived so long, but I never have found anyone like you. Me! She was truly startled, I not in any way special. Oh but you are! She laughed a genuine laugh of mirth. How do you figure? All the dragons feel the same way, he said, they have a intense respect for you. That's because I married their leader, that's all. No, not so, ask them and you will find out. They respect you because you respect them. You are mature past your age and also you treat them like your equal.

You may not know it but most people treat us like animals or pets or some kind of abomination. They fear us or loath us. Men feel like they can't compete with us and women are afraid they will give birth to a monster. They have almost never loved us. There was one exception though. Tell me, she prompted him.

Silvia, he said, his face relaxed and his eyes got a far away look in them as he remembered. She was a black haired, olive skinned, daughter of a tavern owner in a little town in Spain. She watched me land and change one stormy night. She was totally convinced that my ability was something I could give her. She was going to tell people who and what I was, I couldn't find a way to stop her until I told her I would pay her to keep her silence. I was living in a small cottage in the woods and spent my time hunting and fishing and selling the extra to the local merchants. I paid her what would now amount to four dollars a month. She was happy, but came to see me regularly asking to be made into a dragon, I never convinced her I couldn't do that. As we talked during the times she came, we grew to be friends. One night she caught me naked in the woods by the cottage getting ready to change. She was down wind on a breezy night, I suppose that is why I didn't notice her approach. I was going hunting. I had noticed that she had been hinting about bedding me, I didn't want her though, it was a time in my life that I wanted nothing more then to be alone. When she saw me there she took advantage of the moment, we made love in the woods there on a pile of leaves. I came close to falling in love with her, she died with some fever less then a year later. I moved to France, I didn't want anything to remind me of her. What was she like as a person? Tamara asked. Very free spirited and superstitious, she was funny also. I knew her a little over a year. Right after I came to America I came across a young man that I worked with in a mill, we became friends. His father became ill and I moved to his families farm and helped them, I had a short affair with their daughter. No love involved, she would bed anything, I thought maybe even her brother. I went to work for a surveying crew, the government ways paying, the

government wanted to expand the territory. I met Leslie hunting
one night. We gathered together any dragons we came across,
you know now how to spot one of us, we could find our kind
even easier.

It took quite a few years but we soon were four. One of
those was William, he was young. He had been born to a dragon
father and a woman he had fallen in love with. I know from that
there were dragons in Europe but I never found any. From what
William remembers she didn't love his father and fought him so
that he held her captive until William was born and some time
after as well. Both of William's parents died in a fire before he
reach puberty, he had it rough when he reached puberty, no one
to guide him or help him. He came over on a ship as a mate. He
was full of ambition and was the one to get me interested in our
future as dragons, but it was Leslie that really inspired me. We
hadn't mated in a very long time. We all have bedded women
along the way, but not mated. There might be some dragons from
the affairs out there. As best we can guess sometimes dragons can
procreate without the circle but it is some what rare. We realized
our numbers were small and we had stories of our kind being killed
by mysterious men trained to hunt us. We made a league, and the
next time one of us could mate we found a woman, someone that
would not be taken seriously if they talked about it. We mated and
we began to build our numbers up. It took a long time as many
times the women didn't carry to term, at a certain point, I think
it is at eight of us, we found out we absolutely had to have the
circle to procreate. When we would get above about fifteen, things
began to happen to some of us and our number was driven down.
We began to believe the stories of men that were dragon killers
and began to protect our selves. Now you have come along and
we are appreciative. That's fairly much it in a nut shell. You have
to realize that in times past, the rush and hurry you feel in these
days didn't exist. Priorities were different then. Also you spent a
great deal of your time in survival, it was a good deal harder to
live. We were in less of a hurry then most people because we had

longer to live. She had watched him and listened to his history with great interest. So this was him, a man with knowledge of so many years, housed in this twenty something body. It gave him a charm that was irresistible to her. She had watched as he had relived his past, the changes on his face as different emotions passed through him. His angular features showed emotions from anger to happiness, contentment to sorrow, but every time he looked at her she saw happiness. She took his hand, Acacia, that was special to me, I feel like I know you better then ever. You have a dimension to you now that has been expanded for me, not like a photograph. He smiled, you will tell me your story then? Yes, she smiled, next time I'm on top. He really laughed, you've never been on top. That's right she said, getting up and taking his hand they walked toward the resort.

The next property was perched on a hillside, a winding road hugged the mountain and ended at a plateau that according to the paper work was ten acres, the total was thirty five acres including the part of the mountain that would be theirs. This she liked. We could make this our base, Acacia said, build a good ops backed up to and a little into the mountain. It's fifteen minuets to a main road and twenty minuets from a highway. It's not so high that it would get really cold and there is only a small chance of snow. If it was fenced properly, it would be a good place to raise the children, Tamara said. They used the key they had been issued to unlock the gate, and drove up the road to the plateau. The plateau was almost naturally flat and covered with the brown grass of late summer. It was straight where it backed to the mountain then made a big curve out and back to the mountain with the road coming up from the left if you stood looking at the side of the mountain. Acacia peered off the plateau, power is right there at the road, the well would have to be down there and pumped up here, that's doable. He looked around with a satisfied look on his face. They drove to the motel where they were staying, and freshened up for a early dinner. Would it be expensive to put a good fence around the plateau? She asked him. No, not to expensive. I would want fruit trees and grapes, she said. If the other dragons are going to get married, we might just have cottages behind the main house, she continued, thinking out loud. Would we have enough money for everything? She asked. He smiled at her needing to worry so much, yes, we should have enough. How long would it take to build a home here? Two or three years I would suppose. Do you think the other dragons will like the plateau? She asked. I think yes, He said. I didn't take pictures, I forgot. She was disappointed, he could tell. Let's go eat, then we can browse the sights. When we fly out, we'll stop there and take pictures. The restaurant was great, a large square fire place was in the center of the room, flames rippled across it. The food was the best she had ever ate at a restaurant. They strolled some of the old streets of the town, then went to rest in their room and talked.

Chapter Twelve

They flew out just before dawn and landed on the plateau, he changed and naked he began to explore the top of the plateau. They had brought a picnic lunch, and some miscellaneous tools, they measured and marked and laid out a house, a pool, tennis courts, putting green, pond and seven cottages. They spread a small blanket and she stripped down, and they made love in the middle of the plateau. At dusk, after they had relaxed for a few hours, he changed and they were again in the night sky. The third property was a complete dud, they drove the rented car around it for a while but nothing about it drew their interest. They looked it over for half a hour and drove to the house and to Annabelle.

The pictures turned out well, and they were all setting around the dinning table discussing what they would do next, as the pictures were passed around so every one could see the property that Acacia and Tamara were interested in. There are about sixty more properties we have on a list that the real estate agent gave us, Acacia told them, do we need to look farther? This does look good for security, William stated. The freeway access is a good one as well, Alexander said. Well I don't really have an opinion, Ben said, and Susan feels the same way, if everyone likes it we will also. I like the property, Albert said. I say we go for this one, Brock agreed. It would be hard to beat the location, Roman said, I definitely like the difficulty in accessing the property, the power lines going through there are a big plus. I'm good with it if the others are, Timothy said. I'm ok with it also, Forest said. Me too, Peter said. I just want a better infirmary, so it's good, Leslie agreed. The next thing is financing, Acacia said, We can easily buy the property out right. But to build the compound we want, and the ops center we need, would cause cash flow issues. I estimate about fifteen million. A ten million mortgage until we could sell this place, is there any reason not to sell this residence? Then we would pay it off? Asked Roman. We could not pay off the mortgage until the new one is built and we move and this is sold, it will take about three years to build, so we have a mortgage of about three and a half years start to finish. We have no other mortgages, our annual intake is about eleven million. Net on that is about six. We have about eight in cash but if we get the property that would leave us with about three for operating expenses. That keeps us in good shape, William said, if we all agree we could put an offer tomorrow. I see they're asking three million for the property, we should only offer two, Alexander said. Most of them agreed to that. What should be our final offer? Acacia asked. No more then two and three quarters, Leslie said. Everyone agreed to that. Acacia recapped it all and they all agreed to it, the meeting adjourned.

You know them better then me, Tamara asked him when they were alone, what did they really think about it. They were all upfront, it's good for all of them. We do this every seven to ten years, we have gotten used to it. It is important enough, but it has also become routine to us. He stopped talking and looked at her face, oh this is a project you would love to oversee, am I right? She smiled at him. Yes, Acacia, yes very much. I'll talk to the dragons, but I have a feeling they will be very relieved to not have to be very involved in it. You will have to get their needs from them on any part that has to do with them, like the set up of the infirmary and ops and the like, but on the whole they will probably be appreciative of someone to take the project on. It turned out they were very happy for her to see to the projects oversight. The escrow closed in a little over a month, and she had already set down with the architect for the first consultation, after going over the plans with the dragons, she was to meet with the architect the next morning for the next step. She made the changes in the plans that the dragons wanted "the architect was very helpful," and he said she could pick up the final set in three weeks. She had went with a classical architectural look with columns all about it, columns lined the pool area and along the walks to the out structures. She had had Kevin, who was the architect assigned to their project, put in a lot of detail into the exterior facades, and the interior as well. She had gotten good news from him today, the cost he had estimated would be about twenty percent lower then they had anticipated. It was partly because she was going to, with the architects help, oversee the construction, so she headed back to the dragons with the news.

The bad news came a few days later, their enemies it seemed had learned from them. The accountants had called, someone had brought the IRS down on top of them. They had requested a good number of files from everyone of their companies, more then an ordinary audit would have requested. Acacia assured Tamara they would be ok when she expressed worry, I keep good books and the companies were on the level. It was going to cost them in time and money but that was all. It would tie him up personally, he warned her, I don't want you getting frustrated. Two weeks later the architect called, she could pick up the plans, he was submitting the plans and application with the county the next day. He was going to grease the wheels in the county a little, he believed they would have tentative approval in about two weeks, he would call her then. If you get that for me she said I'll send you and your wife to dinner on me, anywhere within reason that is. She, on the architects instructions, called the concrete contractor and gave him notice to be ready to start soon. A little over two weeks later the county called for her to come pay the permit fees and pick up the approved plans. She called Acacia and announced they were starting.

The new place was a little over an hour dragon flight from their current residence, she was planning to ask the dragons to take turns flying her there and home again maybe two or three times a week. She was purchasing a used double wide and having it placed on the property as an office and living quarters. Acacia was going to fly in as much as possible to see her and Annabelle. William got wind of the plan and shot it down, he was insisting that she have two of the dragons stay there as well.

Tamara was excited, Alexander was going to fly her to the construction site before dawn in the morning. She had the double wide all ready and only needed to stock it with supplies. Susan had gotten wind of what she was doing and was coming in a few days, she was going to bring a vehicle for them to use there. Roman and Forest were coming to stay with her and do any manual labor and keep her safe, she welcomed it all. She had helped her father in his construction business and had wanted to build something herself some day, well today was that day.

On the roof top the dragons stripped down and changed. Roman and Forest went first, they carried some things she needed for the next few days. Alexander caught her by the shoulders and they were off. They arrived at the jobsite about ten minuets before dawn. She handed Alexander his clothes from her pack, then gave the others their clothes and they went into the trailer. I would like to have this room if it is ok? She asked the dragons. There are two other rooms over there side by side, they share that bath. Every one seemed happy with the arraignments as they went to their respective rooms. She was expecting a delivery truck in a few hours, in the mean time she would be dealing with the concrete contractor. The architect, with a little bribing, was going to be a quality control consultant.

Tamara had a few minuets before they were to arrive and she went out to look around, there was one place standing at the edge of the plateau that you could see out over a beautiful valley with a good sized creek running through it. When Kevin arrived she would talk to him about a small platform protruding a small ways off the plateau. She watched as two trucks came up the road toward their drive and turned in. The truck were loaded with long boards, she knew they would be the concrete crew. She watched as they made their way up onto the plateau. A silver Mercedes came into view and turned into the drive, that would be Kevin. Almost two hours later there were stakes with white flags all over the plateau and they were finished with the first stage in the layout, the concrete crew would take it from there. The men from the concrete crew had unloaded their trucks, and the trencher they pulled behind them was beginning to start trenching the main house. Kevin had taken down the dimensions she wanted for the observation platform and was leaving.

Two weeks later Susan and Tamara with Annabelle and Cameron were driving up the drive. It was a Monday morning and they were coming to the building site for the week. The concrete for the house itself was finished, the framing crew was coming this morning. Stacks of lumber that had been delivered days before, were sitting ready for them. The framing contractor was an older gentleman, he was friendly and was full of good information. Roman and Forest had flew in, they were doing some clean up of the site and were cutting down a tree and trimming another that were in the way of the framing. The concrete crew was coming back tomorrow, they had some concrete to pour for the out structures. A salesman was standing by his car waiting, she had gotten used to them they came by from time to time trying to sell her a product for her house, most of them had been of no interest to her a few were. She waved him into the trailer as she and Susan stepped in themselves. Susan took the children and put them into bed, they would finish sleeping for a few hours. The man walked up to the desk as Tamara slipped behind it. What can I do for you? She asked him. Tamara is it? She stopped putting away a paper into a drawer and again she said, what can I do for you? I am not here to sell you anything, I here to warn you of something, with those words he had her full attention.

Do you have any idea of the history of the creatures you are dealing with? She looked subtly out of the window trying to see one of the dragons. She prayed in her mind that Susan would stay in the other room for a while. Fear gripped her spine as he continued. They are a vicious evil creature that can kill without giving it any thought. They are murders, power hungry murders, they want the annihilation of every person that is not of their kind. They are using you and when their number it twenty four they will discard you like the daily trash. When all of the children reach puberty they will have the power to make you do what ever they want and even make you like what it is they decide to make you do. We will not let them get that power, we will destroy some of them at least to stop them, take your child and go far away. You have been warned. We know all about all of you and you will not be spared after today. He walked out as Susan walked into the room.

Tamara rushed out and came upon Roman first, Roman that man driving out is one of them, he just threatened me. Tell Forest, he said, as he rushed behind the trailer. She heard the sound of his wings as he flew off diving off down the drive out of view of the workers. Finding Forest she told him and he was airborne in moments following Roman. She called Acacia on her cell phone and told him. I'll be right there he said. She knew the dragons were taking a great risk in flying during the day, she was really worried. She knew they wanted to find where the others operated from, she just hoped it was worth it. They had found it before, but the fires they had set had only stalled them. They wanted to do more damage this time, that is if they ever found them again. She filled in Susan about what happened. Who are theses guys? Susan asked. While she waited for Acacia Tamara told her all she knew. You have been safe but coming here changes things a little, I had thought that it was over after Roman was shot, Susan said. Mostly yes, but it looks like they are planning to step it up. Why do they hate us so much? It's a long standing feud over wrongs from long ago, Tamara told her. The thing is, I believe that the dragons have changed for the good a good time ago. You know them, they wouldn't hurt anyone if they didn't have to. These others still hold a grudge, this guy right now didn't even give me a chance to talk. They're really serious, these others, they really tried to kill Roman, we have to be careful.

Acacia dropped down outside the trailer, Tamara went out to meet him. He hugged her, you ok? Yes, just a little scared. I've asked Ben and Albert to come and help you, I don't need them for what I'm doing and they can keep an eye out for you both, I'm sure Susan will like that. Yes, I'm sure she would. He picked up the clothes he had been carrying and slipped into them. What are you going to do about your next job, will you all be safe? She asked. The next one is about a month away, we'll work it out by then. Now tell me exactly what happened. Well he talked about the long ago, the past, the one you told me about. He asked me to leave and go far away, he threatened to kill Annabelle if I didn't, and swore you would never have the power that the twenty four will give you. What is this power you both talked about? He said you would be able to make me do anything you wanted, and I would even like what you made me do. Is it true? He took her by her shoulders, yes it is, it is a very great power, if at any time you feel I shouldn't have it you come talk to me. Think it through, decide if you feel if you can trust me. You have until the children all reach puberty, I will accept your decision, what ever it is. If you say yes, I want you to be my conscience. Help me, keep me on the right path. How will I know you wouldn't be manipulating my mind. I'll figure something out, maybe you could write what you think down and compare it with how you think later, we'll work it out if you will please be patient. Think about it, I don't need to think about it, I trust you, I need you. There was a moment of silence between them.

Acacia? Yea, he whispered to her. Thanks for telling me the truth, the man didn't tell me anything more then I knew from you, I think that surprised him. I know, Acacia said. I felt good about that, you had told me the truth and I was ready for him. Tamara? Yea, she whispered into his ear. I need you also, he said. She hugged him. Roman and Forest landed beside them, he went to a mall in town, he could have come out anywhere. We didn't want to be seen so we came back. We need to step up security, Acacia said, but how I'm not sure. We could all go somewhere and stay, Roman said. For ten years? Forest said, it would be hard. They know they have ten years, they have been careful up until now, what will they do when they have a lot less time? Acacia said thinking out loud. You guys better get into the house and get dressed, he handed them the clothes he had picked up while he and Tamara had been talking. And thanks. They nodded their acknowledgement and stepped into the house. He and Tamara walked in after them. A few minuets later Ben and Albert walked in holding their clothes in their hands.

All of the dragons hit the refrigerator and food, the changing having made them all very hungry. She still didn't know how they stayed so calm, she was shaking earlier, now she was calm because they were here and she felt safe. I'm going back, Acacia said to Tamara, I'm already rested, I'll see you when you come home on Friday, we'll discuss this more when you call me tonight. Ben and Albert brought some weapons, you will be ok with them. I'll get you better fortified tomorrow. Tamara asked, how can you be so calm? We have dealt with this many times, you never have, I'm really worried about you. Tamara hugged him, I'm really angry, Acacia said, that's why I'm so calm my right now, a man just came onto my property, threatened me and my family and my friends. I'm not a violent person, but I could do the some damage to that man if I could find him. I think, we should hire this project out and get you and Susan and the children back where we can protect you properly. Let me think about it for the week and we'll talk about it, Tamara said, Ok? He nodded reluctant agreement, and she watched as he slipped out side to where the workers couldn't see him and stripped and changed, he flew off staying just above the trees. She went out and picked up his clothing and brought them inside, then she busted up laughing. The others were staring at her, I'm picking up his clothes behind him already, and she busted up again.

Chapter Thirteen

It was the weekend and they all were having one of the planning meetings. We need them here where we can watch out for them, Roman and Ben were saying, we can't have them spread here and there, we know this property and how to defend it, Ben added, he reached and took Susan's hand. The children, all twelve of them, were playing in the corner being unusually quiet. They all were walking now and it was hard for one person to keep up with them. We are building the house because we need to move, Tamara said, when we get done it will have the best security that we could get, it needs to be finished as soon as possible. We can hire a contractor to finish it, Albert said, It's not that we don't have confidence in you, it's because we care about your safety. Tamara was tired of all of it, It would have been fun, but with a threat looming over them all of the time, she was ready to give in. I will concede to what ever you people want, besides you're right it will be easier to hire it done and Susan and I can focus on the children's education. Acacia came over to where she was setting, Tamara I really appreciate this, if we didn't care, and not only for the children, we wouldn't be this way. You and Susan are our family, we all have appreciated both of you being here, we couldn't bare to see anything happen to you. She patted his hand on her shoulder, I know guys, she looked them over, it's just I really was really going to enjoy the building, it would have been fun and a real learning experience. We are all agreed then? Acacia asked. Everyone nodded they were. Tamara you and Albert can call the contractor we used last time, see if he is available, would you do that? Sure she said smiling at him, sure.

The next day Susan came to her, it was the right thing to do, she said, let them keep us safe, I see how Acacia looks at you, he really is in love with you. Yea, Tamara agreed, like a fairly tale, you feel the need to pinch your self. It's like that with Ben also, he's so gentle with me and that look in his eye when he comes to me, well you know. You think it's because they have been without someone to love them so long? Susan asked. They know how to love, Tamara said, never controlling, never pushy, there when you want them and busy somewhere else when you need space, it's uncanny. I think about what that man said to me, I don't know what he was trying to say. Do you think they can read our minds and they're not telling us, Tamara asked her. No, Susan laughed. Well you know the old saying though, if it's to good to be true it probably is. You over think, Susan told her. What if they do get the power that they told me about? Tamara asked. Susan looked at her for a while then she said, he told you first didn't he? Yes. Well he didn't hide it from you did he? No. That says a lot, Susan said, has he manipulated you in any other way that you know of? No, no he hasn't. Well relax a little bit then, besides, she said, if anyone was to have control of me I want it to be Ben. Tamara laughed at that, your right, I believe Acacia really loves me so I shouldn't be worried. We need to find the room we want for a class room she said, let's go find one. They made girl talk as they checked different rooms, they came across one, it was fairly large and completely empty.

If we put the chairs here, Tamara said, walking a rectangle. Then the windows would be to the back here, and the blackboard here, she concluded, gesturing toward a wall. This closet would be perfect for storage, and a few shelves, Susan said, it would be perfect if we had an exterior door.

Tamara turned and looked at the windows, easily done I think. We should go find some chairs online and also a blackboard. Are we starting to get this ready a little early? Susan asked. Yes, Tamara said, but I'm bored and need something to get my mind off things. We need a big party, Susan said, something wild, she continued. Like what? Tamara felt the mood she had been under for a while start to lift. I don't know, what do you suppose the boys would like? They need to relax, they don't drink heavy because of security. I think girls for all of them besides Ben and Acacia, Tamara said, but I don't see any way to work it out and still keep good security. What if we went online to a dating service and choose some girls at random? Susan said, set them up for a date, do a background check, then we could hire a security service to guard the perimeter of the grounds, it would work as long as we had a way to make sure none of the.. We need a name for those people, how about killers? That works for me, Tamara said. We need to make sure none of the killers get on as security. We will also need to sell it to Acacia as well. We could have a lot of food brought in, set up some huge sound system, have an open bar. What if we hire a chef and a bartender? Tamara asked. If we do a good background check on them it should be alright. What about money? Susan asked. I check with Acacia.

Acacia really didn't like the plan for the party, he was worried about so many new people in the compound. Tamara asked if William could go over everything and then they could get together and work out the details. That will work, Acacia said, if William says ok I'm in. There is one more thing, Tamara said. Ok, Acacia said cautiously. I want to be trained in the use of a gun and some of the training you guys get for your work. What training? He asked. The training that will help me to keep myself safe. Acacia thought about it a second then said. I can have Brock work with you on all of that, he is the best at most of what you are asking for. But you have to listen and learn, he has no patience if you don't put your whole heart into it, he'll kick you out. I'm serious, very serious, Tamara agreed. I'll listen and learn, don't worry. What brought this on all of a sudden? Acacia asked. I just realized that I have no idea what to do if I'm attacked. That man threatened me, my daughter and my husband the other day. Acacia, he didn't offer to talk or anything, he just said he would do us harm! Acacia I will be ready, if they do try to do any of us harm, I will kill them no questions asked. Acacia looked at her, good, this is the place where I needed you to be but had no way of getting you here. You are safer already. Brock will start working with you tomorrow. I'm very happy you came to understand the gravity of this. Changing the subject here now Acacia, Tamara said, if there is any way we can work it out about the party I would love it. Susan and I really want it to work out. Acacia shrugged, we'll try. She hugged him, thanks. She watched as he went back to what he was working on before she interrupted him. She moved around to look over his shoulder, what you doing? She asked. Diagramming a plan for a job we have been asked to do for a client. I need to know if this plan is doable before I give them a price. She watched him as he worked, when he stopped for a moment she asked him question. When is this supposed to go? She asked him. About nine months from now. Can you teach me what you are doing here, I want to learn how to do this part of the work. He hesitated for a moment. Is this a bad time to ask? No. he said, this is perfect, I could use the help. I'll start you with the basics.

Chapter Fourteen

Brock had her meet him in the gym the next morning. We will get you in better physical condition as we teach you some of the basics of self defense, he told her, you never know what you may need to do to get out of danger. Being in shape is essential for many other thing you want to learn as well. We'll also go to the range and get you started on the basics of guns and also their care. After that we will start on attack strategies and hand to hand. A little later we will start you on using a knife but that can wait a few weeks.

The aerobics and the weight lifting were ok as far as she was concerned. When they started the gun training that was when she really started getting tuned in to what he was saying. Acacia had warned her, Brock didn't take nothing less then a total commitment to what they were doing. When he sense her mind wondering in the least he immediately did something to get it back, and it wasn't something pleasant. She learned how to hold a gun, how to take apart and clean a gun. She learned the sizes of guns and how this made a difference in their use and how she had to handle them. Brock mixed verbal instruction with hands on instruction, this made the lessons quite interesting and they never seemed boring at all. He had a good sense of humor and they teased back and forth. She found him to be a sweet warm hearted person.

After two week Acacia showed up at one of the training sessions where they were working on the proper stance while shooting. Brock was repositioning her when he walked in. How is she doing? He asked Brock as they stopped to greet him. Tamara went up to him and gave him a kiss. She is attentive and has learned fairly fast, Brock told him, she is having a little trouble with shooting stance and with breaking and recovering from falls, and also with handling rifles. But the problems are small, mostly a matter of practice. Acacia smiled at her, that is really good news! She felt herself flush with appreciation. Acacia didn't give out praise unless it is deserved. Brock was one to speak the facts about her training also. She knew she was doing good, and that made her day. You want to come to ops? He asked her, William has some very interesting information, we all want you to be there for the meeting. Brock had slipped out of his clothing while they had talked, and was headed for the showers when Acacia called to him. Make it quick Brock, this is very important. Brock waved his hand in response. I need a shower also, Tamara told him. Make it real fast, he said swatting her on the bottom, every one but you and Brock are already there and waiting.

The dragons were seated all over the place in the ops, chatter was coming from all corners as Tamara walked in. She seated herself by Acacia and it immediately became quiet. Acacia taking some papers stood and passed them off to be circulated among the dragons. We have come across some information and strangely it was by accident that we discovered it. By this information we now believe that the man in this picture A mister Tim Pierce, is the top leader of the ring that has attacked us over the years. If this information proves to be correct, we are looking at the person responsible for the deaths of many of our colleges and friends and even our children. We have agreed to keep no secretes from each other that could in any way bring harm or the chance of harm to any of us. I am giving you this information because I trust each one of you now, and have at times trusted you each with my life. Having said this I must also say we do not need a vendetta started concerning this man. We will find the indisputable truth and then pass appropriate judgment as a group not as an individual. I need each ones verbal commitment to this. We are stronger as a group, we are smarter as a group and we need each other. So, by a verbal aye, and a raised hand I ask for this commitment, when I have this I will start the planning. Hands went up and they all made their commitment. Thanks for the vote of confidence Acacia said.

Let's start with ideas first, how do we find out if this is the person we think he is. Albert spoke up, ask him. There was several voices of agreement. Next Alexander suggested they spy on him and follow him, some more of them agreed with this. Acacia wrote this down along with the first suggestion. Any other ideas? Acacia asked. We have this information by financial records, William said, if there is any other way of confirming it that one of you can think of, please speak up. After a time and no one said more Acacia went on. This man is quite wealthy, he lives in San Francisco. He heads more then one international company, doing business mostly in the manufacturing sector. He will have excellent security measures. We will have to be extremely careful with what ever action we decide on.

It was decided in the end that they would try to get him to talk first. They would use fear and coercion, they would use his family or whatever it took. We should track him, Peter suggested, follow him and learn all his habits. We could even get a good surveillance device and use it, that way we run less of a risk to ourselves. There is no reason to try to keep it secret from him,

Peter added, the more we stir him up the more we will find out anyway. Roman spoke up agreeing with Peter, we should stir him up, make him nervous, get him to reveal more about himself. If he feels threatened, said Albert, he will either act guilty or not, either way it will help us assess the truth. Anyone else have any more ideas or anything to say? Acacia asked. When they all had nothing to add he went on, we will work on a plan and then have another meeting to finalize it. If anyone comes up with any more ideas let me know.

Most of the dragons filed out of ops leaving a few behind. How are you going to do it? asked Tamara. I'm not sure yet but I thought one of us could fly into his compound, hold him at gun point, put some fear into him and query him. We could see that he is by himself and not able to call for help. Some of the others will keep the guards at bay by keeping them busy, it should be fun, I will see if anyone else come up with a better idea. Acacia, promise me you will let someone else talk to him. He smiled at her, I knew you were going to say that so I had William pegged as the person to question him. Besides he will go farther then me to get what he wants. Thanks, she hugged him. Who else do you think might be going? I am going, William, Albert, Alexander, Roman and Forest. I will be running the whole thing from a van. William will be questioning him and the others will be pestering the guards keeping them busy. I'm going to man communication here in ops, she said. Good, we need a good person at com, there will be a lot of coordinating to be done. When are you going to commence operations? We will have to all agree then we would need a week at least to get all of our groundwork covered, we have to watch the place, get the guard's schedule down. We will find a place to set up the operation, it really shouldn't take much more then a week. A few days later they were back in a meeting, they all listened as William laid out the plan, little by little with every ones help they tied up loose ends. Within an hour they had a workable plan that all of them were comfortable with. They were going to put it into action Monday after next, that was gong to give them plenty of time to get in all the info the wanted. Tamara could sense the excitement among them as they thought of the preparations. She was excited as well, but with more apprehension then the dragons.

Tamara worried about the children more then she probably should, they were all walking and talking. She and Susan were starting them on their letters and basic math, the children were incredibly smart and were already progressing farther then she had expected. She had the dragons prepare a place in ops for them so she could keep them by her and Susan when the dragons were away. She didn't worry when they were all down in ops together, she felt safe there.

Tamara was concentrating on the conversations between the dragons coming from her head set. Acacia had told her it would be a busy night and she had been frantically trying to keep up with the action. She listened to the chatter and tried to keep each one informed as to what was going to happen next and to keep them informed as to what had already happened. They relied on her to give them updated information, she had to be up to date and accurate to do that and that required her complete attention tonight. They had located their target in the master bedroom of the pent house he occupied at the top of one of his buildings. A short time before they had dropped some flash grenades at the main gate drawing the majority of the guards to it. She listened as Albert reported that William had landed on the balcony and was breaking into the French doors. Next he reported that William was in, having broken down the doors. Acacia asked her to warn him to watch out for a body guard that might have went to get the target to safety. Albert reported that there were two other people besides William in the room but the situation looked under control. After a time, the others began reporting that they couldn't keep the guards occupied for much longer. Acacia asked them to do what ever they could and keep them up to date. Albert reported that William had changed to human shape after hitting one of the two with his tail. How many people do you see? Asked

Tamara. Two right now, one of them is William, he answered. You sure? She asked. Absolutely, he answered. In a few moments Albert reported that William was on the balcony, he's changed and he's airborne. Help me get them all out of there Tamara, Acacia called to her. Tamara worked frantically to get all of the dragons pulled out and in the air in three minuets, I'm on my way back Acacia, reported, I want a meeting when were all there.

Chapter Fifteen

They were again all gathered in the ops for the meeting to talk about how the action had went. The buzz of excitement filled the room as many of the dragons felt that they had made considerable progress in relieving themselves of the people that had worked so hard in destroying them. Acacia stood up and when he did the room quieted. As you all know the operation went as we had planned. William was able to speak with Mr. Pierce, he seemed a reasonable man and has agreed to respond to our request of a chance to negotiate a peace between us. He has said we will hear from him in three days.

Now William will answer any questions you may have about what Mr. Pierce had to say as he was the one that spoke to him. William took up answering questions, Acacia took up a seat beside Tamara and Brock took a seat on the other side of her. Brock leaned over so only they could hear him, there is something wrong here. Tamara agreed, they have been trying to destroy us for a few hundred years now, why would they agree so readily? Because in three days they have something planned against us, Brock said, I'm sure. Acacia looked thoughtful, that is why he said in three days, not within three days. Acacia stood up and when William had finished answering a question he interjected his own. Did Mr. Pierce have to think about his answer when he told you in three days we would get a response? William thought for a moment, no not at all. Well then Brock and myself propose that they will be attacking us on the third day. He capitulated easily, and knew the time already, there is no other explanation that fits, we're being set up in a way.

Alexander spoke up, they are expecting that we will be complacent, waiting for the answer from them, not at all ready. That's right, Acacia agreed, but we are not going to be. William would you get a plan together? Sure, William said, I'll have it ready for tonight. Ok let's call this meeting finished but we all should get back together when William is ready. Tamara, you come with me if you would, I want to see to a plan for the children. We need to work out what we are going to do with them to keep them busy down here all day. I already have some ideas, Tamara said, they will have lessons for one thing and if we move a screen down here they could watch a movie or two. Then we could give them some dance lessons as well, tire them out if you know what I mean. I'll move some painting supplies down here as well. Acacia laughed, sounds like you have it all figured out, I'll go help William. No, no Tamara said, I'm sorry Acacia, I don't want you to feel like that, I want any input from you. I was just teasing, he hugged her to himself, I want to spend some time with you and Annabelle.

What would she like to do this afternoon? We could take her out to swing, she loves that, maybe the sand box. We could picnic out under the tree. That sound so good, he kissed her long, I'll get the blanket and toys for Annabelle, you want to see to some food? Yes, she said, Acacia was happy to see her face light up. She took his arm, let's go get Annabelle from Susan.

Tamara woke to a fuss just outside the bedroom door, she looked at the clock by the bed, it was just after four a.m. she got up and put on her robe and opened the door. Acacia and William were standing and talking quietly, Acacia turned to her, just some small last minuet decisions, he said, I'll be in, give me a minuet. Tamara closed the door and went to get a shower, she suspected Acacia would come and shower in a moment. She was about half finished when she heard the door close and after a moment he stepped into the shower. He hugged her and kissed her good morning and washed her back as was his usual practice. Get dressed for work love and we'll get started moving the children. She moaned as his strong hands rubbed her back as he washed her. Ok lover, she said, I'll meet you in the nursery then.

They were waking the children four at a time walking them to the elevator and down to ops. They had fixed them all pallets and organized an area for them. It was still early and all of the children seemed to be ready to go back to sleep. Most of the dragons were now taking up places around the grounds and building, getting ready for whatever might be coming. I hope we are so wrong, Tamara said more to herself then anything. As I am also, Acacia said, but the more I thank about it, the more I'm sure we are not.

It was about seven a.m. when it happened, it was just getting light out when they busted the gate down with a black SUV. Others came toward the house from all directions, they all had silencers on handguns and rifles as none of them could afford an incident with the local police. Tamara stayed in ops helping the dragons, she was doing her best to keep them up on what was going on. Susan was watching the children in the corner that had been readied for them. She could hear the thwat thwat of the guns through the radios, as the dragons reported what they saw and warned each other and organized their movements. Tamara's heart fell when Peter was cornered by gunfire for a moment. Albert and Roman helped him out of trouble, but they were forced in closer to the house because of it.

The battle was going for about half an hour when Leslie was wounded and they had a hard time getting him into the house. It was left to Tamara to tend to him and grabbing the first aid kit they had ready, she went to him in one of the outside bedrooms. He had a small flesh wound that she bandaged at his direction, I'll be just fine he said taking some pain medication. She had just made it back to ops after tending to Leslie, when she heard Acacia call for assistance, he was pinned down, Tamara could hear the alarm in his voice. She grabbed her gun off the desk and telling Susan she would be right back, and went to help him. He was just outside the gym behind a pillar, but there were two gunmen keeping him there and he had seen another one moving in to get a shot at him.

Tamara's heart was racing as she tore through the house to get to the window in the gym. She had a radio on her side and she heard him as he reported that the third gunman was getting close. Brock was trying to get to him but it was taking him a while as he was taking fire also. Tamara, after what seemed to her like a life time, finally made it to the window. She lay down on her belly in front of the window and slowly raised her head up to see above the sill the way Brock had instructed her. It was a good thing she did as a bullet shattered the glass a little above her head. She ducked and rolled a little to the side of the window her insides shaking. She had never been shot at before and was shocked at how unnerving it was. She was breathing hard as she raised up to look again. It was perfect timing as she saw the man that was coming for Acacia moving along some plants, Acacia shooting at him as he moved. Tamara took careful aim with the pistol, sighting down it with care and breathing slowly as Brock had taught her, she squeezed the trigger.

She was sure she was off the shot as she was in a hard position but the man fell just as he was starting to run across an open area, stumbling for a second. She was horrified for a second then saw the movement of one of the other shooters, he was getting into position to shoot her husband. Acacia caught her eye and she knew what he wanted. She took careful aim again, this time at the shooter she had spotted earlier by a tree. To her shock she hit the tree close to his head, Acacia took the instant and leaped to cover beside her, laying on the ground under the window. You ok? he asked her, concern thick in his voice. Yes, she was barely able to get the words out, I think anyway. A shot exploded the casing of the window, Tamara heard herself scream a little scream as Acacia flattened himself against the ground. Tamara saw a flash of color outside the window as Acacia having spotted the last shooter, had sat up quickly firing three shots in rapid succession and had lain back down. Tamara watched as the man he had fired at clutched his leg in obvious agony.

Tamara screamed again as Acacia unexpectedly dove through the open window. She got out her third scream as another form came diving into the room through the window, tackling Acacia. She knew in an instant it wasn't a dragon and she spun around kicking the figure in the side, satisfied with the sound of cracking ribs. The man rolled off and she saw the mans gun pointed at Acacia's side and she realized she had just save her loves life. Her own gun came up and her shaking hand pulled the trigger at the same time she saw the flash from the mans gun and the jerk of Acacia from the impact of the bullet. She had shot the man in the shoulder just as he had pulled the trigger and shot Acacia. She raced over to the man who was holding his shoulder and kicked him in the nuts, she was satisfied to hear him scream and then he fainted.

She rushed over to Acacia searching his side for a wound. Then she saw the blood coming through his shirt and grabbed her radio. Acacia has been shot she said as she keyed the mike on the radio, I'm going to need help in the gym, I'm not sure how bad. She stopped talking as Acacia called her name, she realized then she was sobbing. She leaned down to him, shush honey, some one is coming to help. Leslie came rushing through the door, he kneeled down and whipping out a blade, he sliced open Acacia's shirt cutting through the blood stain. Tamara saw his shoulders relax as he examined the wound. He keyed the radio and announced to them all that he would be just fine the wound was minor. Tamara started crying again but with relief, then Leslie called to her asking for assistance in getting him to ops. She was happy to get busy and they working together helped Acacia to his feet an they walked him to the elevator. He winced with each step, but soon was walking on his own clutching his side. I'm going to dress the wound, but don't worry it is a surface wound, the bullet passed through the flesh, didn't even enter the abdomen.

William came on the radio, Timothy and I are tying the prisoner up, we're going to put him in the garage. Have them tie him both hands and feet, Acacia gasp. Leslie nodded his head in acknowledgement, passing on the instructions. Tamara could see the strength returning to Acacia and was relieved. In the ops she watched as Leslie examined and then bandaged the wound. The others had reported that they had turned the attackers away, beside the prisoner they had a body to deal with, it seems that the man Tamara had shot in the leg had bled to death, having tried to crawl away, the movement expediting his demise.

When Tamara and Acacia was alone, he kissed her long and hard, thanks for saving my life, if you hadn't shot him he might have shot me in the heart, that's where his gun was. They heard Ben come on the radio, you need to come to the garage and check the prisoner he said to Leslie, he's bleeding from the groin. Acacia turned to the intake of Tamara's breath. You did right, Acacia hugged her to him, you might have saved both of our lives. Leslie was tending the man Tamara had kicked when they arrived in ops. There was blood all the way down the man's legs, Leslie, a man with a good heart, was sewing up the man's sack, he look at Acacia, I thought about not anesthetizing him so you could interrogate him while I sewed. But he was in so much pain that I didn't have the heart. Acacia asked Alexander to bring the dead man down to ops, we'll see if we can get him to identify him when he wakes up.

After a short time Alexander and William came in carrying the man. This is Mr. Pierce I'm quite sure, William said. Well when we get this guy awake we'll have him identify him to be sure. How is he going to come out of this, Acacia asked Leslie? He will probably be ok, but there was some major damage to both of his testicles, she did a number on him, it's possible he could have a low enough sperm count to be considered sterile. When will he wake up? About thirty minuets, he'll be hurting really bad unless I give him something, Leslie explained.

We'll give him something when he answers our questions, and only then, said Acacia. Ok, Leslie said turning to walk away a smile on his face. The man talked all right, in between begging for pain medication. The dead man was the brother of Mr. Pierce, but they also found out that they had all but eliminated the group Pierce led, it was down to a ragtag few. The dragons had called in all clear one by one while Leslie was tending to the man, and now they were all down in the ops discussing the events of the morning. Tamara was getting more and more embarrassed as they came to her telling her how good she had done. Susan who had been taking it all in was telling her she was proud of her. I heard you on the radio, you did really good. Acacia stood up to talk, we need to get off an attack on them tonight, they won't be expecting us and we need to put an end to this. We tried to deal with them in good faith, I'm tired of it, rage filled his voice. They all agreed. We need a plan, said William, let's get it worked out.

Chapter Sixteen

Tamara set at communications, it had just turned dark and the dragons were reporting in ready one by one. The plan was to all change into dragon form, and get into the buildings by breaking windows using large steel object they had taken with them. They would use accelerants and light as many fires as they could and get out, they were going to burn down the buildings, there was to be no mercy. They had to be in and out in ten minuets, that was the time they expected until the police and fire could arrive. They all circled above the building, when Acacia dove they all followed, ten minuets later the occupants of the compound were all dead. They had ripped some of them up and tossed them into the burning building. Some they had set on fire, breathing fire on them. As for Mr. Pierce, William had taken him high into the air and dropped him into the fire. They had flown away to the sounds of the approaching sirens.

That night Tamara tried to comfort Acacia but he was in misery, I never wanted the dragons to be like this, I thought we could avoid this kind of violence and work it out like civilized people. This is the same place that the dragons were at a thousand years ago. Not the same place, she disagreed. You have been attacked, you defended yourselves, you did not initiate the offence. Acacia, this is our children, you know that they have killed your children in the past. She watched as Acacia ran his hand through his hair, he had been pacing as they had talked. You told me that you wanted me to be your conscience, keep you true when you have the power, well I'm keeping you true now, you did the right thing, I'm telling you, you could not keep on letting them attack and kill you. He stopped to take a long hard look at her, you really believe that? You have no doubt in your mind? No, I'm sure of it. Listen Acacia, they have hunted the dragons almost to extinction, who has the right to do that or to even make that decision? Your right, he sat down on the side of the bed. Your right, we have the right to survive, he held his head between his hands resting his elbows on his knees. I love you, you know, Tamara went on, I love Annabelle the same way I love you. I'll tell you right now, I'll do anything to protect her from anyone. No one is going to take her from us, not now, not ever. You with me or not? Acacia took a deep breath, I'm with you. I just hate the killing, it really gets to me. Well when you get the power, this killing is going to stop. We will see to it. But until then we do what ever it takes, right? Yes, he was standing up tall now. You need to go out there and tell the dragons they did good, she explained to him, you go encourage them, make them understand they did what you wanted and what was needed, they need to hear that,

She followed him as he went to the library where the dragons were gathered. As he entered the room the soft talking slowly died away. I have never been more proud of you men as I am now, he started. You have done something very difficult for anyone who has morals, but what we did was just and it was right. We have been hunted to the verge of extinction by people who have tried to be judge, jury and executioner. We shall continue to stand for our right to live, he raised a fist into the air, now let's celebrate! He watched them as they broke into cheers and the party started, Tamara was right he needed to be more committed and quit feeling sorry for himself.

He woke the next morning to Tamara shaking him gently, he clutched his head and moaned. Sorry she whispered, but you have to see this. She pointed the remote at the TV and it snapped on. She adjusted the sound and he was able to catch the last of a news spot and the very fuzzy picture of a dragon in flight in a night sky. Some one got a picture she explained to him when he looked at her in question. They are supposedly checking it now to see if it was faked. Not to bad news he assured her, this has happened before a few years ago. It seems to be more then any person can believe so they always write it off to something they can't explain. She visibly relaxed. Sorry to wake you then. No, he said, I need to get up, he move to get out of the bed and moaned. You want an aspirin? She asked. Yes, he gasp in pain. Well lay back down, she instructed, I'll bring it, and she left the room. When she returned he asked her how the children were and who had helped her with them last night? Susan and I managed all right. She smiled at him as she handed him the aspirin and a bottle of water to drink. You guys were up until four this morning, she told him. What time is it now? He winced as he turn to look at the clock by the bed. She took his face in her hands and kissed him, time for you to lay back and let the aspirin take effect. Everything is ok, you relax for a while, I'm going to go for a second and when I get back we'll shower. He nodded his head in acknowledgement and lay back gently on to the bed. Be right back she said slipping out of the door.

Acacia began to remember what had happened at the party and cringed, he was always sorry when he drank heavy, well they needed it he supposed, and he was probably not the only one regretting his actions, he thought to himself as he thought about some of the things that William had done. He chuckled and made his head hurt, and Roman also must be sorry for drinking so much. The door opened and Tamara came in with some coffee and a few rolls. The coffee smelled good but the thought of the rolls turned his stomach. Tamara who seemed to him to be mature ahead of her time, coaxed him to drink some coffee and then had him take a bite off a roll. After a few bites he was feeling better and ate the rest of the roll. Your to good to me, he teased her. She brushed back his hair with her fingers. I always felt I would find the right person one day and that is why I never dated much and never slept with a man. When you saved me off the ledge and landed beside me I seemed to know you were the one.

The new house will be finished next month, Acacia told her as they lay under a tree Annabelle playing with some of the other children on the grass close by them. A little less then eight years and the children will be reaching maturity. We will be able to have another one, Tamara's eyes lit up, I wonder if it will be a girl or a boy? They both turned a shouts came form the direction of the house. Brock came rushing out of a door and ran down the side of the house. Albert was right behind him shouting obscenities as he ran. Acacia shook his head and said, "not again." Not again what? Tamara asked Acacia, concern thick in her voice. Acacia lay back onto the grass, they do this every so often, they get into a big fight sometimes they even go to blows. Tamara jumped up when she saw that Albert had tackled Brock. Acacia pulled her back down to sit on the grass, leave it be, one of the guys will split them up if it gets too bad. Are you sure of that? She asked. I don't see anyone with them. Acacia started to rise letting out a sigh, I suppose I should go see to them. Tamara stopped him with her hand, Leslie is there now, he is talking to them. Tamara jumped up, damn! Albert just hit Leslie. Ok there's William, she went on, there they all go, they're all running now. Acacia pulled her down to sit with him again, forget it they'll take care of it.

William came into the ops where Tamara, Acacia and five of the dragons were sitting around the room. William was sorting through the mail, a letter for you Acacia, some name I don't know, William told him as he handed it to him. Tamara looked over his shoulder as he opened it and began to read. When he had read a short time he sat up straighter. William who had been watching him stepped a little closer. What is it Acacia? This is very interesting, Acacia said as he read the rest of the letter. We seem to have a friend that we didn't know about, he told William, at least I think so. He set the letter down on a desk, this letter is from a person who claims to be the person that came onto the property those few nights. They want to have a meeting with me, they want to talk. They claim to want to possibly join us. Is this person male or female? William asked. We agreed that only dragons could join us, William went on, if they're female then they could be a mate. It isn't clear if they are male or female, I think I should meet with this person, Acacia said. William placed a hand on his shoulder, it may be a trap. Yes, but this person has set no rules to this meeting so you can come along if you want, bring the other dragons if you want. Where are you to meet? Asked William. A small bar in town tomorrow at eight, if we agree, we can call and leave a message at this number.

William pulled a phone from a holder and looked over at the paper and keyed in the number. Do we call him? Acacia asked. I say we do, William said, we need to know all we can about this loose end. Acacia looked around at the other dragons looking for an opinion from them. They all agreed that it was a good idea to meet with this person. Call them then William and tell them we agree, Acacia said. They all waited as William made the call and left the message that they would be there at the meeting. I wonder who this person really is, Forest said into the quiet that had settled in as they all had gotten lost in their individual thoughts. I wonder why they have been watching us? Roman added. We should know more tomorrow, William said as he turned to the elevators, I have some things that need to be prepared by then if you will excuse me.

Tamara and Acacia followed him to the elevators and they all stepped in. In the elevator as they road up, William spoke to

Acacia, I would like to take your place if you will let me. There is a good chance they will not know what you look like. Acacia thought about it for a moment, no I think I will go, I feel no real threat from this person. William nodded his consent, very well then, I'll get together those who want to go, we'll be ready.

Chapter Seventeen

All of them had piled into the vehicles and were almost to the bar. They were excited to find out who this mysterious person was but also they all had never been together at a bar to just have fun. They all jumped out upon arrival and filed through the door of the bar. Acacia saw a smile light up the face of the bar tender as a large group of customers filled up the mostly empty bar room. He became very busy as the orders came in. Acacia looked around the room, looking for the person that he was supposed to meet. There had been only five people in the bar as he came in, two couples and a single man setting alone in a seat that faced the door. Their eyes met and it was apparent that the man was the one he was supposed to meet.

Acacia and Tamara slipped into the seat opposite of him, his mannerisms made it plain he was somewhat fearful of them.

Acacia, trying to put the man's mind at ease, stuck out his hand so the man could shake it. They shook hands and Acacia said, you wanted to talk? The man looked around the bar, are you all here? Yes all except one, he and his wife stayed behind to care for something. The children? The man said. Acacia looked into the man's eyes. Yes, Acacia's voice was threatening, are they in danger? Not from me the man said. Tamara took out her phone and dialed Susan. Acacia listen to her as she asked Susan if all was well and then told her that they were fine when she asked. Acacia spoke and asked the man what he wanted to talk to them about. Oh! Tamara said. Acacia looked at her in question. You're a dragon Tamara told the man. He turned questioning eyes to her, yes I am. Acacia understood, you are looking for your people, do you have any knowledge of your past? Some, the man answered, I know I am a dragon and I believe you are as well. I was raised in an orphanage, a really nice woman that worked there, one that I consider my mother knew I was different but she cared for me, raised me and protected me. She passed away last year, she told me I should look for others like me, she had wanted me to have friends like myself. I just happened to be driving out at the desert one day a little less than a year ago, I saw you flying out there and tried to follow you back to where you lived. I lost you when you had gotten close to your home. I have been looking in the that area for a while, that's how I found you. I wanted to meet you and find out what kind of person you are and here I am.

Well it is nice to meet you, Acacia said, we do allow dragons to join us but you have to agree to certain rules, we will have to investigate your background. Are all of these dragons? He asked Acacia. Yes they all are dragons, Acacia answered, we will be happy for you to join us if you are who you say you are, you will like being around your own kind. Would you tell us your name? Tamara asked. Hayden, I was dropped off at a police station as a baby and they called me John Doe, but the women at the orphanage called me Hayden Jones instead of John Doe. I had it changed on my birth certificate a few months ago. You run an interesting show there at your house. I was in special forces, I learned a few tricks from there as to how to foil some of your security measures, the dogs were a good idea though, I didn't know quite what to do. Hayden chuckled, it was then I decided to get in contact with you.

Tamara leaned toward him to hear better over the noise in the room, how old are you? I'm twenty five almost twenty six. Your only twenty five? Asked Acacia as he leaned closer as well but more from a new interest. Hayden seemed to get a little offended, I'm young but I have a good deal of experience you could use in your business, Hayden responded. Acacia sat back, is this what this is about, a job interview? Hayden's face reddened, I think it is time for me to go I need to be some where, he said, as he stood up to leave. Tamara gave Acacia a look as she placed her hand on Hayden's arm stopping him short. Please for me will you sit back down for a minuet Hayden. Would you guess Acacia's age for me? Hayden sat back in the seat, a questioning look on his face. Maybe thirty, he said. Tell him how old your are Acacia. Acacia looked at Hayden, Tamara could see in his eyes he now understood. I'm two hundred and sixty one years old with a birthday coming up. That's not possible, Hayden said, no one can live that long. Dragons do, Tamara said, and longer. They were all quiet as each one partook of their own thoughts. I never knew, Hayden said, no one told me. There was no way for you to know, Tamara said, no one to tell you.

She went on, were you just looking for work or were you looking for more then that from us? I guess I was a little forward with you, Hayden said to both of them, it was just incredible to find someone like me. I had guessed that there had to be others like me but I had doubts if I would find them. I never thought we live longer then normal though, that gives me a lot to think about. Would you like to join us and work and live by the rules we have established, Acacia asked. Hayden looked at him a while, that is what I came here to talk about but I don't know your rules or anything about you to be blunt, I would like to know more though. If it is all right with the others we could have you come to our place and we could talk more about it if you like, Acacia said. I would like to introduce you to the others here if you would like that. Yea, I would like to be introduced, Hayden agreed. Well then if you would like, stay a while and get to meet the boys and the drinks are on us for tonight, Acacia took Hayden's hand and shook it, I look forward to our talk then. He took Hayden around to William and introduced him to William then started to introduce him to the others as Acacia made his way back to sit by Tamara.

What do you think? Tamara asked Acacia. He is a dragon I'm sure of that, Acacia said. But as for the mystery of his birth, that bothers me. Could it be one of our boys? I really don't think so but I don't want to leave any possibility out, Tamara said. As far as I know probably not without a circle, and we have not had any circles with him there. I suppose it could have been a rouge dragon, Acacia said thinking out loud, but how did the girl get pregnant without a circle? Something is not right about this he went on. I feel something is not right or we don't have all the facts as well, Tamara said, but I don't think he is a problem either, he seemed genuinely surprised to learn of your age and think about growing up being a dragon all alone with no dragons to be with you or help you, well that would be difficult I suppose. They both watched as Hayden settled down into a group of the dragons and soon they were all talking and laughing. William looked over at Acacia and spread out his hands asking "well." Acacia just shrugged.

Chapter Eighteen

Hayden was coming to the house in a few hours, they had watched him for a week by constant surveillance and he had done nothing more then work, date, and play video games on his computer. Acacia hadn't changed his mind about him at all, Tamara and most of the dragons were of the mind to let him into the group and give him a chance William Albert and Timothy were leaning toward being more cautious. In the end they all had agreed that they would make their decision after today.

They had planned a fun day for all of them, they were going to have a barbeque, a base ball game, the pool would be ready and if they wanted a late night football game. Hayden drove up in a nice navy blue sports car and all of them went out to meet him as he drove up to the house. He knew most of them by name from the bar and they all greeted him with enthusiasm. William and Acacia gave him a short tour of the house and then brought him out to introduce him to Ben and Susan and the children. Tamara watched him with the children as they each introduced themselves to him. He likes children she noted, but has had little dealings with them as he was awkward around them. She noted as well that he fit in best with the dragons that acted close to his real age. He really got along well with Brock, Peter, and Alexander as they were no better acting then teenagers and it was only a few minuets before they were laughing at some funny thing one of them had said, it reminded her of her high school days. She did notice one important thing about him and it was the way he took everything in that was going on around him. She was very sure he was looking for one particular thing and he hadn't found it yet.

Acacia came and sat beside her and watched her as she watched Hayden intensely. What is it? He asked her. He is looking for something, she answered not taking her eyes off of Hayden. Acacia started watching Hayden as well. After a moment Acacia said, your right his eyes keep looking around, he is searching for something. Cameras, said Tamara, he is looking for cameras. Sure as hell Acacia said after a moment. Are there any out here asked Tamara? One, but I doubt he will find it. Where is it asked Tamara? It's on a tree behind us in a squirrel hole. I have to look for it even when I know it is there. He is still looking, Tamara said. This changes things, Acacia said, I was correct about him. Maybe Tamara conceded, I want to talk to him alone for a little while if you don't care, said Tamara, she stood up. No, go for it, Acacia said. Give me a little while, she said as she strode of toward Hayden. Acacia watched her go, good luck he said under his breath.

Tamara walked up and watched as the three dragons talked. Hayden was still looking, and with every chance he had he searched the area. Tamara walked up to him and asked him if he wanted to set a while with her and Acacia. Sure he said congenially. As they walked toward where Acacia sat Tamara bluntly asked him why he was looking for cameras and watched his expression. He never missed a beat as he told her it was a habit from the service to always look for not only cameras, but shooters and suspicious people and potential bombs as he had served in Afghanistan for two years. Why are you watching me he asked? Because I love my family and you are an unknown, she answered him. They had stopped walking and were facing each other. I approve of that, but what do you have to fear here in America? Tamara made one of her rush decisions. Because since I have been married to Acacia I have had my life threatened, I have been shot at, and my family has been shot at. She was surprised when that statement took him by surprise. Who would do that and why? A man by the name of Pierce. He did it because he and a group he formed hated me because he hated dragons. You have proof of this? Hayden asked. Some Tamara said, we should have some video feed and we have some financial documents that elude to his funding of the group.

This Pierce guy, do you know his first name by chance? No Tamara said but I could probably get it soon. I know a Samuel Pierce, Hayden said but he wouldn't do anything bad to anyone, I had an interview to go to work for him. It was good talking to you, Hayden said, he turned back toward the other dragons and walked away. Tamara went back to sit by Acacia. What did you say to him, Acacia asked. I asked him why he was looking for cameras and he told me it was habit form the service. She looked Acacia straight in the eyes and he also told me he had interviewed with a man called Pierce a short while back for a job. What else did he say, asked Acacia? Nothing, that was when he went back to the others. He is not looking for cameras now Acacia said. Tamara watched Hayden for a while, no he isn't is he.

Hayden was with a group as they were picking sides for a baseball game, he was totally engrossed in the events he was partaking in, a whole different person then a few minuets before. They had chosen six player teams, Acacia, Tamara and Susan had positioned themselves to watch. Roman was out in the center field as he was the one to cover most of out field. The three dragons that were covering the bases were a little in the out field to help him. The dragons strength made it a little different to play as they could hit the ball about a third farther then a man could. They watched as the dragons played and as far as they could tell Hayden never looked around in any way that was different then the others, Tamara did notice Hayden was a very good baseball player.

That night they lit the fireplace and all of them settled around for a chat as Susan passed out beers for everyone. After the conversation had been going for a while and Hayden had seemed to be comfortable William asked Hayden what it was like in the service and how he had been able to get past all the medical exams and blood test without them finding out he was a dragon? What do you mean? He asked. William just looked at him for a moment. If they tested your blood they would know by it you are a dragon. They took my blood but they never said there was anything wrong with it. William stood up and walked over to him, could I see your arm? Hayden held out his arm and William took it and moved it to see the light play across it. He took out his knife and after asking permission used the tip to poke Hayden with it. Hayden bled at the prick.

William turned to Acacia, you seen? Acacia was already up and coming to them, yes, he said. They had all seen the sparkle of dragonskin, but to so easily have been made to bleed, that was not normal for a dragon. The room was quiet as Hayden asked them what was going on. We're not sure said Tamara as she moved over to them, dragon skin is tough and not easily damaged. William would you show him your skin, she asked him. William held out his arm and using the knife sliced down his arm the blade barely broke the surface of the skin. Hayden was staring at it. When did you first change? Asked Acacia. Change? Hayden asked I can't change into a dragon if that's what you mean, I was hoping you would teach me how to change like you do. I watched you all out on the desert, I hoped you could teach me how to do that. How did you know you were a dragon? Asked William. I didn't until I saw you guys changing and I later seen your skin how it sparkled like mine. I knew then I was like you. I wanted to join you and learn how to be like you. William took Hayden's shoulder, we don't learn to change it happens when we reach puberty. Hayden, Acacia said his demeanor completely changed, would you stay with us for a while? Leslie is a trained doctor and we have a well furnished lab, I would like to get some answers for the both of us. Tamara, seeing the fear come to Hayden's eyes spoke up. It is completely up to you Hayden, if you feel uncomfortable with staying here we understand, you can always come back another time if you like or never at all if that suits you. Acacia nodded his head in agreement. Hayden visibly relaxed, if I stay there is something you need to know first, well two somethings anyway. Well we all want you to stay and feel comfortable around us, Acacia said, so what is these two things?

First I am wanted by the law, and second I came here to see if I could find away to revenge my fathers death on you for killing him. Hayden put up his hand to forestall all the dragons from talking at once, I know now I was wrong about you guys, Hayden said, even though I am not sure in what way just yet. Who was your father then, asked Acacia. Samuel Pierce I was made to believe. William swore. Acacia put his hand up and the buzz in the room died down . How did you know he was your father? Acacia asked. He phoned me one day and said he knew who I was and asked if we could meet. When we did he told me all about my life and even some things I didn't know that fit in with what I did know already and said he would do a DNA test to prove it if I didn't believe him. Ok Hayden, Acacia took her by the shoulders, I may have an idea what is going on but I need time and you to find out for sure. We don't care about your record, that is nothing to us, but we need to be able to trust you and that is where I need you to tell us now, I need your word that we can trust you. Can we? I swear you can trust me, he said looking into each face, I know you are good people and I know when to keep an open mind. I trust you now, and you can trust me. I would like to start as soon as possible, Leslie said, what do you need me to do Acacia?

First we need to know for sure if Pierce was really Hayden's father, we kept some of his blood if I remember. Yes, as we always do, said Leslie. Well then work first on verifying that, then see if you can tell if Hayden was a genetic experiment by Pierce and his group, I think they were children that were started in a lab, that is how they were able to get past the circle. So that is what you are thinking, said William, it makes sense. He is strong as us and has heightened senses as well but he may not be a dragon as we are, they would have been interested in the special abilities with out a doubt. Yes, said Acacia, looking at Hayden, but still they would be our brothers. You think there may be more like Hayden out there then? asked Albert. If there is, said Acacia, we need to let them know they have a place with us if they want it. Hayden spoke up, I know a little about genetics and something like this is not yet possible. But it is, said Acacia, not something that happens very often but it has been going on for a few years now, long enough for you to be the age you are. They have even revived extinct species but they have been careful what news they let out. But I'm twenty five years old, it would have had to happen that long ago, said Hayden. In vitro has been around longer then that, we can mate with humans, the cross over should have been easy. So they were making a stronger army to use against us? Tamara asked. I believe that's correct, said Acacia, but we must have got to them before it had been finished.

How long ago did Pierce get in contact with you? Acacia asked Hayden. About a week before he died. I'm sorry about your father Hayden but we didn't have any choice. We did try talking to him first, said William, I spoke to him my self. He was determined to stop us and kill all of us if he could. Stop you from doing what? Asked Hayden. Stop us from growing as a group, Acacia answered, they have always killed us to keep our numbers small. They have been hunting us for over nine hundred years and that's just my knowledge of them, I don't know how much longer before that. Let's get you down to the infirmary, Leslie said, we'll get those test going if you don't mind. Hayden stood up and followed Leslie as he started off. Acacia and Tamara watched him go, I should have seen it, Tamara said, he doesn't have that perfect look the dragons have, he looks nice, but not that dragon look. Acacia took her by her hand squeezing it lightly, let's go look for a good room and get it ready for him. We could put him in the guest suite Acacia said. If we do he may feel that we are getting him as far away from us as we can, Tamara said, I think a room by one of the dragons is best, beside one of those would be much easier to get ready. Sure, Acacia said, where is one? There is one by Roman's room, or there was a few days ago, I went in it by accident looking for Susan.

Chapter Nineteen

After they had gotten a room ready they made their way down to the infirmary, I gave him a basic physical and I'll do a more though one in a few days. I will work on the lab work tomorrow but as for his blood it is more or less normal. I expect there will be some hormone levels out of the norm but nothing more then that. The DNA test will come back in about two weeks and I have blood from Piece to send with it. Tamara noticed that Hayden had his groin area covered, something a dragon would not have done. He also was uncomfortable with her being there in his state of undress. I am going to check on Annabelle, she told Acacia see you when you get there, you can show Hayden his room? Acacia nodded his affirmative as he listened to Leslie as he continued. The additional strength I expect is going to come from a genetic predisposition to strength in his human genes and his dragon genes. This is going to show up in hormone and liver tests as it puts the body out of the balance a doctor would consider normal, Leslie was saying. It might flag a test for a second look but when everything else in the physical checks out it will probably have been ignored.

How much do you sleep at night? Leslie asked Hayden. I do good on five, if I'm stressed four is better some times. Were you able to out run all of your class mates? Yes, the coach at high school wanted to send me to the Olympics but I hated running. In high school all I ever wanted to be was a solider, I joined the Marines as soon as I graduated, I stayed in school and got my diploma because Sam the lady at the orphanage asked me to. She was so good to me, she was so like a mother to me, I couldn't let her down. If they tried this on others, Leslie warned Acacia, they could have gotten very different results, some might be very aggressive or unstable, so be careful Acacia. We have a room for you beside Roman and Forest, Albert will be just down the hall, you ready to call it a night, Acacia asked him. Yea I'm tired, Hayden said, I haven't played games like that since high school.

What do you think? Acacia asked William. I think you are most likely right about them trying to make a stronger man for some reason. More then that, said Acacia, I believe some of those men that attacked us were part dragon. Stop and think about it, they hate dragons so why not use dragons as the fighting force against us, men trained for free at the expense of our government. That would mean this Sam lady knew what he was and that was why she pointed him toward us in the first place, William said, it makes sense. There is really no way she could have known he was a dragon unless she was told by someone, and that someone would have been the one who made him, the one that finally contacted him to offer him a place in his little army. Yes, Acacia said, it had to be Pierce. We'll place Hayden under surveillance for a time until we deem it safe for him to be alone. And William, Acacia said, this is for his and our protection, we have no idea what Pierce may have planned with this guy. Well you picked the right room to put him in as that room has an alarm that I can set to trigger in ops if it is opened. That and a posted man will do it. Who is in ops tonight, asked Acacia. I will be tonight, I drank lightly for that very reason. Good, I'll come by in the morning then, Acacia said, opening the door to leave. Well good night then, said William, and don't worry. The door closed, leaving William in silence.

Acacia woke to Tamara on top of him, her breast pushing against his chest. He feigned not being able to breath properly and whispered, hey lady you have to get off! Tamara laughed and rolled off him, bet you'll never guess what I want.

William was sitting in ops when Acacia came into the room. Anything, asked Acacia? All has been quiet, William said. I did get the order for next week put together though, it will be nice to get moved into the new quarters. How much is it going to cost us? Acacia asked. Just short of fifty thousand, William said. Well we are going to have to get back to work then after we get settled in, Acacia said. Well that will not be a problem, William showed him a bid request, we have this request for a bid to cover a load of pharmaceuticals for TellGen in transport, about a weeks worth of work, you want to bid it? When is the job? Asked Acacia. Two weeks one day from now. We should have security up and working in the new place by then? I would say with room to spare, William said. Good then bid it, Acacia told him I'll let the boys know. What are you going to tell Hayden? William asked. The truth, and only as much as I think he needs to know. We thought we had stopped the people that were attaching us when we took out Pierce's men but now I'm not so sure, said William, there could be an army like Hayden out there. There is only one way to find out, Acacia answered, we will have to get busy doing research, I'm going to see Tamara now to see if she will get some dragons and start looking into it. I think that is a good idea, agreed William, I would like to increase security to back like it was when we were being attacked if you will allow it. I wouldn't have it any other way, Acacia said as he pushed the button to summon the elevator, tell the boys also that I want all of them to be sharp. The elevator's bell chimed and Acacia walked in, hey and thanks for everything, he told William as the doors close, William nodded his head in acknowledgement.

Tamara was dressed in a nice pair of genes and a halter top and had finished cleaning up after Annabelle from the night before when Acacia walked into the room. Annabelle ran to her father and gave him a big hug, could we play again today daddy, I really had a lot of fun with you and mommy yesterday. I can this afternoon, said Acacia, but me and your mother have a project to do this morning, do you mind playing with the boys for a few hours? Annabelle acted like she was pouting, but Acacia could see she really didn't mind. Off with you then he said, tickling her as she walked toward the door. When she had left and closed the door Tamara asked, "how do you get her to do what you ask so easy?" I seem to have to fight with her for any little thing. I don't really know Acacia said, I just ask her. Well, Tamara went on, I have never dealt with a person who is so sure of what she wants in life, she is just so sure of herself and it is getting harder for me to persuade her to do something she needs to do, even when she has been doing it for a while. Acacia could see the frustration in Tamara's eyes as she went on, she even balked at brushing her teeth this morning, and that just out of a blue sky. Acacia took her in his arms, give her time he said, she seems to be a little older then her true age, it could be a phase she will pass through.

Tamara turned to look into his face, I think she might be infatuated with you, she seems to need to please you. Well we will just use that to our advantage then, the most important thing is to not let her actions come between us, Acacia said giving her another gentle hug, we work together about this, besides being sure of what you want is not a bad trait if it is channeled into productive things. Ok, well since that is settled what was it you wanted me to do? I need you to look for some people. He filled her in on what he and William had decided, see if you can find any orphans that could be tied to Pierce. William should be able to help you get started. Ok, Tamara said, what are you heading off to do? William is going to bid a job we might be interested in and I am going to fill the guys in on it to see if they feel we should take on a job now. What about me? I will talk to you later, there would be no reason to ask you about it if they didn't want to do it right? Yea, she agreed reluctantly, but don't forget me. You would never let me do that I'm sure sweet heart. To true, she agreed.

Tamara remembered something she had been wanting to talk to Acacia about. Acacia what do you know about the dragons old history is there anywhere I could find more about your past. I have told you all I know, he reminded her. But is there anywhere I might find out any more, some old books or papers or family writings? Talk to Leslie, he had an interest in that for a while he might know more. Ok I will, I'm going there now to check up on how the test are coming along. Good, he said, I should be free in a few hours, we'll meet for lunch.

Tamar pushed through the doors into their infirmary, Leslie was hunched over a large piece of equipment. At her entering he looked up and seeing her, jotted some information down and came over to her. What can I do for you? I wanted to know how the test were coming along, she answered. Well I found he has some dragon in him as Acacia suspected, I believe he was right about his suspicions about him being a half breed, I'm just finishing up with the test on Pierce's blood. About that, Tamara said, why did you keep Pierce's blood? We keep the blood of anyone who makes an attack on our property, some years ago we were able to get the police off our backs by using the blood of one of Pierce's men that we had on hand by accident, ever since then we kept blood on hand for just that chance again. It will be ready to look at through the microscope in about three more minuets.

What did Hayden's blood tell you? Tamara asked. Do you know anything about DNA? Some little, Tamara answered. Do you know about the caps on the ends of DNA that limit the number of times it can divide? Yes, I read some about it in biology in high school, she answered. Well, Leslie said, in dragons it allows for cell can copy it's self many more times, maybe endlessly, therefore the person never grows older. That is how I look to see if a person is a dragon or not I've always just checked the blood. Leslie took some liquid out of a machine and dropped some out on a slide, dropped some colored liquid on it and slipped it into a machine. Tamara followed him as he walked over to a small screen on the machine, there on the screen was some small fuzzy looking odd shaped things laying every which way on the slide. Leslie touched her elbow to get her attention away from the slide. What you are seeing makes me know Pierce was part dragon as well as Hayden, I need to tell Acacia. He is meeting with the other dragons right now, Tamara said, he said I should ask you about the history of dragons, that you had studied it some.

Leslie turned his attention to that subject, I do, I have files of information, files of information that need someone to lovingly work on it. Tamara's face lit up, how come you never told me about these files? I didn't know you were that interested. I've been asking a thousand questions of Acacia for a few years. Yea, me too, said Leslie, he has no interest in the history of our kind, I really do not understand him about that. He might be more focused on the now, and on them having a future, Tamara said, and the way things are going it has been good he has been I suppose. Well we both can agree on that, Leslie added. Well, you will find some files in the computer under "Draco" that is Latin for dragon. Also you will find a box in that closet there, he pointed toward a freestanding cabinet that went from floor to ceiling, marked history, feel free to do what ever you think you can to organize them. Tamara sat down at the computer he had indicated, and he walked over to her, do you have any questions before you get into this project? Yes, I can't seem to understand why the dragons, didn't dominate the humans as they are clearly the much more powerful race.

Well I think I may have found that answer for you already, I believe the dragon gene dwells in every human, so first, we are the same race just a mutation, second, the gene used to get turned on every few hundred thousand births, in the last one hundred years it seems to have come on and stayed on in some of us permanently. Understanding came into Tamara's thoughts, the dragons are the coming race, she said. Leslie sighed, I am thinking so more and more. What do you mean by more, Tamara asked. If the dragon gene becomes primary in the way I suspect it will in a few more generations, there will be no more humans left in about three generations after that happens, Leslie said. One more thing, Tamara said, how are you able to change, it goes against the laws of physics, or at least the way I know them. You are right, Leslie said, and I cannot fully explain it so I call it magic. There is no such thing as magic, Tamara retorted, if I were to believe in magic I would have to believe in Santa Claus and the tooth fairy and werewolves and vampires. Well I have a good reason to believe the vampires and werewolves were real at some point in time, Leslie stated as if stating fact.

You have got to be kidding! Tamara exclaimed with a chuckle. They are all over in history, in almost all cultures, did you believe in dragons a few years back? No, but vampires? Tamara was incredulous it was clear. Is it not possible they were hunted to extinction? Leslie said, in retort, after all we dragons were hunted, maybe they were all killed.

Tamara realized that Leslie had turned red in the face. I'm sorry Leslie that I took it so lightly, I didn't mean to say something that bothered you. Leslie paused as if to decide exactly what he wanted to say next. I really shouldn't let it bother me that you didn't think it could be true, Leslie said after a moment, but I have come to believe that it is very possible that they really were hunted to extinction, when we have time I will show you the evidence. Well I really am sorry, Tamara said, I didn't have any idea how calloused what I said really was. I'm sorry also, Leslie said, I should have told you I had some reasonably solid evidence. So let's get back to your job of finding what Acacia needs then, Leslie volunteered as he walked over to a computer, you said it was about orphans? If you go to the state website you can find some information on the orphanages in the area and then from there I will help you get into the websites and data bases to get the information you are after. You know how to hack into the databases? She asked him. I have a program, if they are hooked up to the net we should be able to access them. Ok then, she said, I'll get started.

Chapter Twenty

Tamara was really excited as she took the information that she had gathered to Acacia. She was shocked at how Leslie was able to get in the back door of so many institutions and even some government sites. The information was all there, it was shocking to realized how much information was kept on an individual in this day and age, this experience really had made her uncomfortable. She found Acacia going over some maps and building plans in the bar off the dinning room. I have some of what you wanted, she told him, I can't believe how easy it was to get. Acacia smiled at her, Leslie is a wiz at the computer isn't he. But it was Albert who taught him, nothing is able to stay hidden if Albert gets after it, so if you get stumped see Albert. Ok, and why did you just finally tell me that? Tamara said a little aggravated, you seem to wait to tell me these things later then sooner, like when I asked you about the history of the dragons. Leslie had a great deal of information and I had to find it out by chance after asking you who knows how many times. Tamara was just getting going, she was frustrated, and that voice in her head was telling her to stop that she would regret saying more.

To her own surprise she stopped holding her hand up for him to wait for her to finish so he could have his say. I'm sorry, she said after calming a bit, I went overboard, you have a good deal on your mind. Acacia placed his hand on her mouth, sshh, no you are partly correct, these thing mean nothing to me and I treat them like that, they don't stay with me and I'm the one to be sorry, after all you did ask me a good many times. Now I'm in a hurry so the news can wait a little while if you would please, but as for the history, well you really should talk to all the dragons as they all have a memory of things they were told and things they remember. Now I have got to go, get back to me in about two hours and we can fight then.

Tamara watched as he walked away, he was right, if she wanted to know why didn't she think to just ask. Peter was in the next room talking to Forest, she walked over to them and waited, after a moment they paused talking and looked at her waiting. Would you two mind if later at your convenience we got to gather and I asked you about the history that you know about dragons? That's not a problem right now if you like, said Forest, I have time. This evening is ok for me? asked Peter, when she turned to him. Good for both, she took Forest by the arm and they sat together on a sofa and Peter left telling her he would come see her later in the day.

By the end of a week she had interviewed all of the dragons. Also she was able to give Acacia a long list of names of potential part dragon men like Hayden. For almost ten years, Tamara pointed out to Acacia, there has been an influx of male children into the foster care system and this is for only the area around us. It looks as if someone was letting the system provide for the children and any who survived into adult hood were sought out and asked to go to work for theses people. But if I'm right

I think we will find that many of them went into the military. So Pierce or someone like him would have trained men for all but no cost, Acacia finished for her. Leslie suspects that they mixed the dragon and human genes just enough that they would not show as anything more then human on any medical test, but they would get the advantage of a much better employee in strength and agility. Yes, Acacia said, but to what end? We are not sure, Tamara said, but he believes they get additional strength, endurance, length of life, stronger immune system, and their bodies would be harder to damage and if damaged they would heal much faster, but all of this in such a way as to not draw any real attention to them either. But there has to be a reason, Acacia said, and not just to fight us, so what are they planning? You think they have a bigger plan? Asked Tamara. I'm sure of it, either Pierce or someone else was planning something and the dragons were possibly the only thing that could have stopped them and that is why they were after us.

Tamara thought it over, it does make sense. But what could that be? Asked Tamara as if talking to herself. I don't know but I want you and Albert with Leslie helping as you need him to take any resources you need and get busy finding out. He took Tamara by the shoulders and looking deep into her eyes said, get this project going and get it going fast, something about this really has me worried, I have a really bad feeling about this. Sure, Tamara said, we will get you some answers in a few hours if we can, Acacia, she said, you look scared, I have never seen you scared. I believe they are or were planning to take over the military, Acacia said, and we have no idea how many of these soldiers are still in the military, nor how many of them they may have influence over. If these people that know about us were to take over the United States military, we could be dead in a matter of minuets from a strike and they would just say it was an error of some kind. If you take over the military and you could by threat control the government, well you get the picture. See what you and Albert can find out as quickly as possible.

With Albert's expertise, Tamara had much more information including a complete list of suspected hybrids in the military, a list of how many suspected hybrids decided not to go into the service and they also had their addresses. Tamara felt they had made good progress after an intense day of searching. She, along with Albert, felt that it wasn't as bad as Acacia had suspected as many of the names they had were people that were working for Pierce and many of these were no longer a threat for various reasons. But one thing was certain, there was a good deal more hybrids out in society, and she was sure Acacia would want to bring then into the circle as they had Hayden. Tamara thought about the problems of working with that many new people and how would they trust them. They were to start moving into the new compound day after tomorrow and though it was bigger it could never house the amount of recruits that they would be getting if only seventy percent were to want to join. Then along with that, what Leslie had said about the dragon gene becoming prevalent made what they had to consider incredibly bigger then they had expected. She was looking at the start of the "normal" or "standard" human becoming extinct, she was having a hard time wrapping her mind around that. She also realized that if these new life forms were to be policed it would have to be by other dragons, the problems were growing faster in her mind then the solutions she could come up with. Now she realized that Acacia had been right on the nose when he had asked himself what had Pierce been up to? What had he been up to? Tamara now asked herself, was there someone else working with him that they now had to worry about?

After about half an hour of working the problem, Albert came to believe that a group of hybrids may be at a camp that was owned by Pierce's company. When they took the information to Acacia he immediately had William get together some dragons and later that day they left to investigate. Tamara had noticed that Acacia had been distracted lately and decided to approach him about it. We have a very big job we are getting ready for and it is taking a good bit of my time and attention to prepare for. Do we need the job asked Tamara? Yes, we are dipping into reserves and I get uncomfortable when we do that, was his answer. We could wait to move she suggested when he explained the amount of money it was going to take to move. No, he explained it is much safer there then here and with the children we need that extra safety. Is this new job dangerous? She asked him. Somewhat but not any more then others we have done, nothing I am worried about. Let me get this job finished and we will all get together and find some solutions that we are all comfortable with. But right now I need to focus on the job, you and Leslie can help me by continuing to find any information you can on these hybrids.

The next day Tamara went to see Leslie in the infirmary, a question was forefront in her mind. Leslie, she said, I like Acacia being lead dragon but what made him lead? I mean how did it all work out? Leslie chuckled, have you ever seen him fight? Tamara thought for a while, no not really. Well Acacia will do a lot to stay out of a fight, but if forced into one he will always come out the victor. Also he has always treated us all fair and equal, if we have a dispute we don't go to William or any of the other dragon's we go to Acacia, we know his answer will be fair and equal and he will have looked out for our best interest. That is why we all love and respect him as a leader, he has kept us all going in what we feel like is the right direction. I suppose, said Tamara, when you live as long as you dragons do, it is easy to just let things work themselves out. For myself I feel a sense of urgency, especially now you have pointed out that the dragon gene is becoming dominate, we need a plan. Hey that reminds me, Albert left a note for you before he left this morning. He handed her a folded letter, she took it and opened up the page. He found where the hybrids are, Tamara said excited, I have to see Acacia about this, see when we can go, you want to come? Yes, I would like that, Leslie said, but it will probably be a few weeks until this latest job is finished. He will want to be there himself you know, he has a good sense of these things.

They moved into the new compound, the move went smooth and most everyone was settled in. William was ecstatic with the security measures and each of them had more privacy. Each of the children had a room to themselves and it helped them as they were each at an age where their personalities were becoming evident and conflicts were arising often.

Tamara was in the office when one of the trucks that often delivered packages came up the drive. She had just keyed in the code that let it through the gate and watched as Timothy raced out to meet it. Timothy had gotten to know the girl the first time she made a delivery to them and he held her up a few minuets each time she came by. Timothy was walking around all the time whistling and singing now, and it was the talk among the dragons. Tamara watched as Timothy lit off the van and blew a kiss to the driver as she circled the fountain and started back down the drive. He ran beside the van until it was going to fast for him and then he turned with some packages in his hand and walked to the entrance of the house. He brought a package to the office where Tamara was and handed it to her. This one is for William he said, I'll give it to him. Tamara looked at the name of the sender on the package he had handed her, it was some office supplies. What's her name? she asked Timothy. Elsa, he said grinning. His grin was infectious and she felt herself grinning also. She is an orphan and doesn't know any of her family, he said, she is so gorgeous, funny, intelligent, witty and I really like to talk with her. She hasn't said yes yet to going out but I feel she is warming to the idea. What if she falls in love with me? I could have a wife and family if she is still ok with it when she finds out I am a dragon. If she is the one for you I believe it will all work out like it did for me and Acacia and Ben and Susan, Tamara assured him, I would like to meet her as soon as you can arraign it. That would be so great, he said, I'm sure you will really like her.

He walked out the door a spring in his step. Two days later Timothy came rushing into the ops looking for Tamara. She is coming by to see me on Saturday, he told her. Who, she asked, he had caught her by surprise. Then she remembered who, Elsa! Oh that is so good Timothy. What time is she coming and I'll make sure I'm here. She said she would be off around three so she set it up for four or around that. You want me to do anything? Tamara asked. No just be here, that would be perfect. Congratulations, Acacia said to him, slapping him on the shoulder, Tamara hugged him, she seemed like a great girl the one time I spoke to her. Timothy beamed at the words, to much in a daze to care to consider it might not work out. When he left Acacia stared at the door, he has it bad, he said, everyone in the room muttered their agreement. It would be really great if it did work out, Tamara said, I have that hope for all of the dragons.

Saturday came and Elsa arrived right on time, she was very intelligent as Timothy said. Very nice looking and was fun to be around. She kept them all laughing much of the time she was with them. Tamara instantly liked her, and before long she felt she had known her for years. Timothy was smitten for sure, Tamara took him aside and cautioned him, "quit starring at Elsa so much" she was afraid he would make her uncomfortable and she wouldn't want to make another visit. Elsa was polite and said her good bye after a few hours promising to visit again soon. Do you like her? Timothy asked Acacia as soon as the door closed. She is a fine girl, Acacia assured him, but more important is does she like you? I want to take her out for dinner as soon as I can, maybe I can tell how she feels when we go out, but for now I believe that she does like me, Timothy said. When do you want to make it known we are dragons? Asked Acacia. After a couple of dates I think, said Timothy, so it hasn't gotten to involved in case she doesn't like it. That is a very good idea, Acacia said, and Tamara could see he had caught on to the fact that Timothy was not so infatuated with the woman as to jeopardize their situation, something that had him concerned lately. We will be ready as soon as you want us to be, said Acacia, we will all be there for support and so she will know we are not pulling one on her. Timothy was smiling a big smile as he walked away. Acacia let out a breath, this may go ok after all.

Timothy was standing by the door waiting for Elsa to arrive, they had dated and were getting along well but today she was to be told they were dragons and Tamar expected that Elsa would have to see it for herself as she had had to. She pulled up the drive right on time as she always had. Timothy walked out to open the door for her. They all agreed that he would handle telling her, but that he would do it in front of them all. They all had dinner in the dinning room and had retired to the bar in the library. After they all had had a few drinks Timothy tapped on his glass with a spoon and said he wanted to make an announcement. As we are all good friends, he started, and all our futures are intertwined, I want to say tonight that I really like Elsa and have intentions at the proper time to express them in a greater way. But she has to understand first what she would be getting into and as we respect each other I must tell her our secret to fully show my respect for her. So I ask you to bear with me Elsa and make your judgment of us after we have finished telling you all that we need to, he said the last looking directly at her. I must tell you, he continue looking at her, that we all with the exception of Tamara and Susan are real dragons.

We live far beyond the normal life span and so for you to continue on to get to know me and the rest of us better, you have to know this in it's fullness. Elsa nervously giggled, Tamara went over to her, it is true Elsa and we need to all go outdoors and the boys will show you, ok, she giggled again, thinking no doubt that they all had planned something special for her. When the dragons were out side they all began to strip. This really had her attention and she sobered when all of them stood before her naked. She looked at Tamara and Susan for an explanation. Tamara motioned to the dragons and in a moment they all changed. Elsa screamed and ran for the door, Tamara caught her just as she was opening it and calmed her with a few words. No one wants to hurt you, but out of fairness you had to know about Timothy. Elsa turned slowly to face the line of dragons, why are you doing this to me, this is not at all funny, she said, her angry face turned toward

Tamara. It is no trick, Tamara assured her, I can prove it if you will go over with me to Timothy you can feel him and he will show he recognizes you. I had a hard time as well, so if you need time let me know. If not Timothy would love to say hi to you. After a moment she allowed Tamara to lead her over to the dragons, now Timothy, and only Timothy will say hi to you, you ready? She nodded agreement but didn't say anything. Timothy brought his head down and dragon kissed her on the cheek. This is Acacia my husband, Tamara said as she went over to him and rubbed between his tufted ears, the love of my life she went on and kissed him on the cheek. Now they will change back, you stand right by Timothy and watch. Elsa backed up a little but didn't take her eyes off Timothy. With the mist and soft burst of air, the boys were standing in front of them again with Timothy standing where Elsa was still staring. Elsa fainted.

Timothy carried her into the house and laid her on a sofa, he went to get some water as Tamara fanned her hoping the breeze would wake her sooner. Susan rubbed her hand and called her name and it wasn't long before her eyes opened and she looked around until she found Timothy. I dreamed she said, but when did I sleep and why are all of you naked she sat bolt upright, what the hell is going on? A few of the dragons that had went out side to get their clothes came into the room still putting them on. You didn't dream said Timothy, walking toward her. Tamara stopped him, get dressed first and let's try to talk to her, she said to Timothy, you are making her nervous. Listen, said Susan, stroking her hand, I had a hard time about it also but we are telling you the truth. Timothy can show you again after a short time if you would like. I must have fainted, she said, as understanding came to her. That you did said Susan, first one that I know of.

Other people know you are dragons? A few, Acacia confirmed. Elisha laid back, I need to go to my home now, I need to go home. Ok, Tamara said, give yourself a few minuets as you just fainted so I will not worry about you ok? Timothy came back inside having dressed, he went to her and taking her hand kissed it. She jerked but didn't stop him, I really like you he said, and not telling you would have been an injustice, I'm the same person you knew a little while ago. I'm not a murderer or anything like that, we don't eat people and we live our lives much the same way all people do. Tamara could see her relaxing a little, I married Acacia after I knew, Tamara assured her, I love him very greatly. How do you know he didn't hypnotized you, or do something to your mind? Because I knew I loved him before he had a chance to do anything to me, also they have let a lot of women walk away, would they do that if they could mess with our mind? No, she agreed, she turned to Timothy, I like you a lot as well, but this will take some time. Sure, he said, all the time you need, I've waited for many years I can wait a bit longer. Promise you will think about it seriously please, I never felt like this about another person. She gave a small nod yes. Timothy gave her a small hug as well as Tamara and Susan, they walked her to her car and watched as she drove away.

Acacia turned to William and Albert, quick change and follow her, I'm worried about this one, Forest you and Roman grab a car and go to her address and call me when and if she shows up, here's the address. Brock did you get a bug on her car? Brock told him he did, the tracking is already set up in ops. Ok, dragons we are on this like we were on Hayden until we know what she will do. Hayden walked up to Tamara, you guys did this to me also? Tamara grinned, yes, but only to protect ourselves, we have left you alone after your second visit as we were comfortable that you were no threat, to answer your next question. I guess I understand why you would have to seeing how she responded, he consented. Timothy was distraught to a good degree but preformed as they needed him to, he was to monitor the bugs and he came through for them keeping them all informed of her whereabouts. They monitored Elisha for five days up until the day she made a delivery to the complex again.

Timothy didn't run out to meet her but waited by the doorway. He greeted her and kissed her hand in the dragon way, what did you decide? he asked her. I want to date if that is ok, I want time to get to know you, I haven't made up my mind about it all. We can date, Timothy said, we will have fun, do something that both of us like, I really don't know what you like to do in your time off. I sky dive, she said, I am on a team. Timothy thought about it for a while and then he began to see a lot of neat possibilities for them. Will you teach me? he asked her. Sure, love to, when can we go? I will be free Saturday, Timothy said. Saturday it is then, she said, we have a meet and the team would love to have a new person to teach, it will be fun. Pick me up then on Saturday? Timothy asked. Sure she said as she turned to go to her truck, about seven Saturday morning then.

Chapter Twenty One

They called off the monitoring of her that morning, and Tamara watched as Timothy wondered off in a daze to do his work. If this works out, Tamara said to Acacia when they had time to talk later in the morning, we will soon have all of the dragons with a family. Leslie walked in to the room, hey there you are, Albert left these for you, he said handing her some papers, apparently a friend at the company that kept the books for Pierce's companies owed him a favor, here is a list of employees and all their information, he said you should be able to find your dragon hybrids off these with little effort. Apparently he employed most if not all of them in different positions. Here is a list containing all past and present employees and a category titled security. Tamara snatched the paper from his hand, oh this is great! she exclaimed, I owe him big time, I'll start trying to make contact with the people on the list today. This might take me only a few days and we can get all of them together to see if they want to join our company. She turned to Acacia, where will we conduct the interviews? How about at the old compound? Leslie suggested, if they join they could all be housed there as we train them and integrate them into the company. We will need more work, Acacia agreed, to keep them busy and to earn their keep. You could have them do the lower grade security work, Leslie said thinking aloud, they would easily earn enough to keep them and to keep them busy. There will be family and social issues but we can work most of them out I'm sure, he added. Well let's get started then, Acacia agreed, I'll let William know and get him started on a program for them and to look for more work. Who could help me with contacting the dragons? Tamara asked. I will not be needing Alexander for a time, said Acacia, you may ask for his assistance. Good, Tamara said, she rushed off to find Alexander and ask for his help the papers still clutched in her hand.

Tamara found Alexander putting up some recently delivered supplies in the storage area off of the garage. There you are she said as she poked her head around the door, he jumped and knocked some of the boxes over he was stacking, "sorry" she said, but are you almost finished? About ten minuets he informed her. Well let me help and it will be five minuets, she said, what do you need me to do? He took her to a shelf a little ways down the wall and pointed to some boxes, open and stack the contents into the shelf, he said. Alexander, she said, as she started on the boxes, I need some help me on a project? I have a list of the hybrids that Pierce was using, we want to contact each one and invite them to work for us, will you help? He stopped for a moment and looked at her, sure if you need me, but what are we going to do with a bunch of new recruits? We are going to house them at the old compound until we sell it and William is going to find some low level security work for them so they pay their way until we can find out how they want to work out the issues they have with being hybrid. Hayden wants to be part of the circle and we want to offer that to the others but it will take time and I'm sure some of them will refuse. No doubt he agreed, but they are really not our problem are they? No they are not, Tamar agreed with him, but they are part dragon, and most of the dragons I've talked to want to offer help even if they refuse, don't you? I do but it could cause us a lot of bad problems if some refuse, we will no longer have the secrecy we have had for theses past three hundred years, that could be dangerous, especially for the children. We have thought of that but there is a chance that they all will join us also. How many are we talking about? He asked her. About fifty she said.

Hey, she want on, you know that the dragon gene is getting stronger in the population in general, right? He stopped working, no I didn't. Well it is if Leslie is right and it will be up to the dragons to police the new dragons as they become a greater percentage of the population. We may have a lot of responsibility on our hands, if the general population becomes aware that there are dragons they could get frightened and try to kill all of us off. They both finished and exited the room. Alexander stopped walking for a moment, if that is right Acacia will need the power more then ever if he is to keep it all going along with no big problems, if he doesn't get the power it will be impossible to police the change at all. Of course you are right, Tamara agreed, and we will also need all the help we can get as well, and the more dragons and hybrids we have working with us the better. This is why we need to recruit as many of the hybrids as possible, you with me? I'll help all I can, he agreed as they started walking again.

It was Tuesday, and Acacia had just gotten in when a knock came at the door. Forest was passing by and so he was the one to answer the door. I'm agent Max Barrett, the man said, holding up an FBI badge, this is Zack Long, he also said pointing to the man next to him. Forrest looked them over upon seeing the badges, how can I help you? He asked the one named Max, a white man of about thirty, tall and slim and seemed to have a get in your face attitude. Zack was a some what short, stocky and had intense intelligent blue eyes that seemed to see everything about him. You can help me by telling me who you are, Max said. Forest could see he was itching to be asked into the house so he didn't invite him. I'm Forest, Forest Tillman, he answered him. Well Forest, I want to speak with Acacia Stone. Max stepped forward as if to walk into the room behind Forest, Forest closed the door a little and said, wait right here and I will get him, then closing the door completely he went to find Acacia. William, who had been watching the scene on a monitor smiled as he thought "good job Forest", then he hurried to find Acacia and hopefully meet him before he was able to get to the door. William found Acacia as he walked down a hallway toward the entry. FBI, he told him, and I have no idea he said, answering the next question before it was asked.

William and Acacia opened the door and stepped out onto the entry porch forcing the two FBI agents to step back out toward the drive. I'm Acacia Stone, he said, what can I do for you? Agent Max with a exasperated expression said, may we go in and sit down? No, said Acacia, we are in the process of moving in and have no place for seating as of yet. The agent seemed to get angry, but when he spoke his voice didn't show it, we need to ask you a few questions he said. Well then what can I do for you agent Barrett? We have reason to believe that you may have illegal fire arms and have transported them across state lines, I am in charge of investigating this claim, may we see your fire arms? All of my fire arms are registered with the state and I am a licensed private investigator and also I'm licensed for private patrol and security. You can check with the state for all that and you will also find I have nothing against the licenses as well. We would like to come in and see the firearms if we could, he said again. Do you have a warrant? Asked Acacia. No I don't have a warrant, do you have anything to hide? I have nothing to hide and you need a warrant so good day Agent Barrett. He and William went back into the house.

You made him real angry, said William, you sure that was a good idea? I don't believe the government should be poking around in a citizens business without good cause, and he has no cause, you know that. That is true, William agreed, but now I am asking myself who stirred this up, that is what I want to know. Yea, said Acacia, that is the question. Do you suppose he will get a warrant? If he does we will then know it was something big the FBI was told, we need to find out what it was. Call Joseph and see if there is some way to get that information, and get him in the loop about this, we need to refer all other contact to him so let's call a meeting. He is just a lawyer, how can he find out anything? Asked William. He is the best lawyer I have ever seen, Acacia said, and he has more contacts then anyone I have ever known, if anyone can do it he can. Well ok, William said as he walked away, I know he is good, but that good. Acacia turned to Tamara who had watched everything from the entry hallway, find Alexander and Brock for me and have them meet me in the library. Tamara went to find Alexander and Brock and Acacia went to find the address for agent Barrett.

The four of them met in the library some thirty minuets later, Acacia with Tamara by his side explained to Alexander and Brock that agent Barrett's residence was only two hundred miles away and he wanted them to fly there as fast as they could and break in and ransack the place if there was no one home. If there was someone there I need you to wait until everyone leaves and go in. Go over the place good, find out all you can about him, we'll see what this man was made of. Why ransack his home? Asked Tamara. Just to put him on edge, stir up his life, make him very uncomfortable. We might even get lucky and find out what this is all about, one thing I can tell you is, this is about more then guns, the FBI is after a bigger fish and we must find out what. It is imperative we find out what is going on as soon as we can and get a jump on them. Why, asked Brock, we have done nothing really illegal, at least nothing they should be able to find out about. Your own words are what I am referring to, nothing they should be able to find out about. That shows we are blind about what they are up to as I think we are, in our position we can leave nothing to chance, no you two get going, you have no problem with getting this done right? They both agreed they had no problem. Acacia turned to Tamara, William and I are going to go give these two agents something more important to worry about. We will be gone for a few hours but we'll keep you updated, and I'll come find you when we return. What are you going to do Acacia, asked Tamara. Our agents are going to have an accident, nothing big just some more stirring up, It will be fine I promise.

Peter came in to report that the agents after spending a short time in their vehicle writing had left out the gate and were going down the drive. William, Acacia said, let's go. Tamara watched as the two men slipped out of their clothes, changed and launched themselves into the afternoon sky. She was worried about this turn of events, but decided to trust in the dragons many long years of experience. She looked out of the window where the two dragons had shot into the sky, the two dragons looked like nothing but birds in the distance and then she saw them dive.

The Crown Victoria shook nearly shaking Agent Barrett's hands from off the wheel. They could hear scratching on the roof. Agent Long started from the sudden impact, What was that! He exclaimed. Agent Barrett wrenched the vehicle back into track on the road, hell if I know see if you can get a look! Long was placing his hand onto the button to roll down the window on the passenger side when the vehicle swerved to the right hitting the dirt and gravel along side the road the scratching on the roof of the vehicle came again. Agent Barrett again was able to gain control of the vehicle and get it back onto the road. He took one hand off the wheel and was rolling down the window for Long when the vehicle swerved off the road and the last thing the agents saw was the large tree rushing toward the vehicle before the crash.

Back at the compound Acacia and William talked it over laughing. We haven't done anything like that in quite a few years, said William. No we haven't agreed Acacia, not for what ten years? At least, said William. Tamara was watching them, you two finished gloating and laughing at the mishap of others? You both sure they didn't see you, she asked them. Yes, they both said. And your sure they were not hurt bad? Tamara asked skeptically. Yes they both said again, we checked them before we left they were just dazed a little, they were conversing together. Mumbling is more like it, laughed William. Was it really necessary? Tamara asked for the fourth time. Yes, Acacia said, you will agree later. Forest came into the room, Joseph is on the line and wants to talk with you, he told Acacia. Acacia picked up the phone next to where he was setting and pushed a button. He listened for a short time and then asked Joseph, are you sure? Ok, Acacia said after listening again, we can do that, he said after a time. Pushing the button that hung up the phone he turned to William and Tamara, Joseph says this is big and his source doesn't know what the particulars are but that some of our arrests are imminent and we need to leave as soon as we can get away. All of us, asked Tamara? Yes he said, we are to leave one person that they can focus their attention on and the rest of us are to go. He said go on vacation and leave a number to reach us at but leave the phone that number reaches here. He sounded real concerned, Acacia said, and he has never steered me wrong in these last ten years.

Who will we leave here? Asked William, always planning ahead. Not sure yet, we can ask for a volunteer, Acacia said. I'll stay then, said William, let them do what ever they can to me. Maybe, was all Acacia said. With everyone together Acacia explained to them all what was happening and that Joseph had recommended they all go on vacation until he had time to get a handle on things. What about the children, Susan asked, Tamara voiced her agreement. They go with us, Acacia said, the dragons have moved their children before, we have a method. Who is staying, asked William. I will, said Hayden out of the blue, they have nothing on me and I can lie well, also I am not a true dragon so they test me as much as they want and not find out anything. Hayden turned to Acacia, yes you can trust me to look out for your best interest. Acacia was taken back, paused for a moment, then said, thanks Hayden. Then Hayden surprised all of them, when he said, I never had a family and brothers or sisters and you all have made me at home and that has meant much to me these last few months, I have your back. As the meeting broke up all of the dragons went by to tell Hayden thanks as they left to go get ready. Acacia, Tamara, William and Forest stopped on their way out, Hayden, what are you gong to tell the FBI if they come, asked Forest. That you all were tired of moving and took leave to get away for a few days, he told them, that will be where I stand and know nothing more. William clapped him on the back, great and here is my phone this will be the contact number we leave. He handed Hayden the phone, get the number then set it somewhere in the house, let it ring when you call, let them find it. Hayden nodded affirmative. Well we trust everything into your capable hands then.

When will you be going and how are you going to leave, asked Hayden. Some are already on their way to our destination, and the rest of us will be on our way in less then an hour. Hayden smiled, I see then, well good journey and don't worry about me, I'll have some fun with the agents that come. Acacia smiled at the thought, I envy you then he said, good night Hayden. Good night, Hayden said. Within the hour the huge residence was a silent as a stone, Hayden when he was sure no one was around got busy with the true reason he was staying behind. He trusted Acacia mostly, but there were a few things that didn't make sense. He had accidentally caught a glimpse of the password that William had used a few days before upon accessing files that Hayden had wanted to look at in the one computer that they kept important information on. He went to the office that they kept in the room off of the ops and sat down and typed the correct information into the screen. As the desktop showed up on the screen he realized the mistake he had made, they had taken the information with them and had wiped the computer of all the programs and their files with the one he wanted to see. Of course they would he thought as he hit his head in exasperation, he would have. That was when the pounding at the door started.

He pushed the button that turned off the computer had made his way to the door that sounded as if it would only last a few more minuets before it collapsed under the barrage. He opened the door to about ten men with swat style garments on and weapons, weapons that he recognized from his stint in the army. Step out of the way, said agent Barrett, we have a warrant, he said, here is a copy. And he pushed way into the house. Hayden stood back as man after man filed into the residence and fanned out into the different hallways and rooms. Hayden smiled, almost everything was still boxed and the boxes set in the appropriate rooms, the agents had their work cut out for them. Agent Barrett turned to Hayden, you are who? He asked. Hayden Jones, Hayden said. Where are the other members of the household? Asked Barrett. They have gone on vacation, Hayden answered.

Vacation! Barrett all but shouted then caught himself, when did they leave? About two or so hours ago, said Hayden finding it hard to not smile at Barrett's consternation. Hayden waited for the next question, he only replied to direct questions and only as much as to answer them and no more detail. How did they leave? Asked Barrett. Hayden put his hand to his mouth as in deep thought, I'm not sure, I was busy and they came to tell me they would be going, but I didn't go with them, I don't know what transportation they used, I could check the garage. No, Barrett said, my men will tell me. Again Barrett knew he had been bested and didn't know what to think about it. You have of course a way to contact them in case of emergency? Asked Barrett. Yes said Hayden, this is the number that was provided to me, Hayden handed Barrett the number he had retrieved from the phone that William had given to him and had written down on a sticky note. Agent Barrett took the number and slipped it into a pocket.

After a short while the other agents began to report back to Barrett that they were alone in the residence. What exactly are you searching for asked Hayden. Barrett only smiled at him, giving no answer. Do you have any idea how long you may be here, asked Hayden to Barrett, I am getting hungry and would gladly make coffee for your men if you would like. You may go find something to eat, Barrett told him, but don't leave the residence. Wouldn't think of it, said Hayden and headed for the kitchen and the sandwiches the dragons had purchased for themselves during the move. He heard William's cell phone, the one that he had placed on the bar like it had been accidentally left there, as it started ringing when he passed down the hall, and then the footsteps of Barrett following the sound.

Hayden allowed himself to smile, it was going well. Hayden let his mind wonder onto the missing data he had wanted to view on the computer. He should have expected that they would take it so the FBI wouldn't find it if they took the computers as evidence. He desperately wanted to see the information, there were some things that Acacia had told him in the past few months, that didn't mesh with the information he had been told about his past. He wanted to investigate the information for himself without interference and with no one looking over his shoulder. He liked the dragons and felt at home with them and trusted them for the most part, but he needed answers if he could get them. Hayden went to the refrigerator and pulled a roast beef sandwich from the huge stack and the thought hit him. If the agents were to see the sandwiches they would surmise that the dragons intended to be at the compound to eat them. He looked around for a place to hide the stack of sandwiches so the agents wouldn't find them, then he thought about how silly he was being. He had told agent Barrett that they had gotten tired and had decided to take the vacation trip on a whim, the sandwiches didn't matter. He was nervous he realized, something he hadn't experienced in his life much, and he realized also he was nervous because he had something on the line, that something was a family he cared about. He did really care about this dragon family, his dragon family.

When the dragons returned he would just be upfront with Acacia and explain the things that were bothering him. Agent Barrett came through the door bearing William's cell phone. Hayden pushed the last piece of sandwich into his mouth and smiled at the agent. Would you or your men like a bite to eat he asked him. No, the agent said, but thanks. This phone rang when I dialed the number you gave me, how convenient. He placed the phone down onto the granite counter top that lay between him and Hayden. Hayden picked it up looked it over and pronounced it to be William's phone. And you have no other number for any of the other members of this commune, asked Barrett. A commune, Hayden chuckled, I hadn't heard that word in so long. I only had the number for the old residence Hayden said with truthfulness. He had not needed any other number as he had just gotten acquainted with the dragons and had been physically with them since. Strange how he had been so comfortable with them and was just now noticing it. He had been by one of the dragons side all of this time and had not needed a phone number. He had dialed Acacia's number to set up an appointment to see him in the beginning but never stored it in the phone, it was long gone by now. He had a family, one he trusted more then he had realized. It felt good to realize it, also he realized that he needed to trust them more, he vowed he would from now on. Barrett had been watching him, is there something you want to tell me, he asked? No, except that you will find that these are good people and you are wasting your time. Yea, well, thanks for nothing, Barrett said. It is the truth, Hayden said to his back as he walk out of the kitchen area.

Chapter Twenty Two

Hayden meandered around looking for a comfortable place to sit, he was tired from the move and frustrated with the agents as they went through the rooms and rummaged through the contents. They were making a mess of the place and for nothing, Hayden was sure there was no gun running going on with the dragons. How could something like this get so mixed up, Hayden knew it was not really easy to get a warrant to search without at least some evidence.

Acacia sat down beside Tamara and watched the children playing on the playground equipment. They were about fifty miles from the new residence as the crow flew but almost one hundred if you drove it. It had been a short flight and no problem for the dragons to make even with heavy burdens. They had booked the rooms at the resort by twos, using Joseph's credit cards as to not raise any traceable money trail. Acacia had told them all to have as much fun as they could and be prepared to stay for at least two weeks. His words had been taken to heart and the dragons were having a great time of it. Where are the boys? Asked Tamara when he brought her another drink from the bar. They are rafting, he told her, they will be back about dark, Susan went with them and that is why we are babysitting all of these little monsters. They are really having a great time, she said, maybe we should have done something like this sooner. Maybe we should have, Acacia agreed. I wonder how Hayden is getting along? Acacia said to the air. He's a big boy, Tamara said, he'll be fine, but I am happy you care. That is something I really admire about you Acacia, she kissed him on the neck, you care for those you come across and not just dragons, she kissed him again.

Acacia's phone rang, he flipped it open, yes Joseph. So they are already there, he said after listening for a short while. You see them, yes, no, just look out for Hayden. No, you will know him he is the only one of us there. Thanks, thanks, yes, bye. Joseph is at the residence, he says there are quite a few agents there, and for me to leave it to him and let him handle everything. Also it seems that agent Barrett was in an auto accident, there are some question of how it happened. Also that he was not able to perform his duty for two days because of it, that is why we had time to act before the warrant was served. Apparently he had went before a judge and the judge had given him a warrant. He was unable to serve the warrant until he had been cleared for duty by a doctor. Acacia smiled triumphantly. Smart ass, Tamara said. He kissed her gently and she knew what was on his mind. Susan will take over watching the children when they all get back, Tamara said, we'll have some free time then.

Barrett rushed to answer the door when the bell chimed. I'm agent Barrett with the FBI he said, flashing his badge at the man who stood there. Hayden watched as the man produced an envelope form his briefcase and handed it to Barrett. Agent Barrett opened it and then began to read it intently. Then he and the man at the door conversed for a little and agent Barrett spoke into his radio, and few at a time all the other agents showed up at the door and exited. Agent Barrett turned to Joseph, I have a message for Acacia. Tell him he does not frighten me. Tell him I do not know how he did it but I am sure now he had something to hide and I will find out what it is. Agent Barrett turned and stepped out of the door. After the last agent had walked out the door, the man came inside and shut and locked the door and turned to Hayden. Joseph Ensley, he said as introduction, Acacia's lawyer. Hayden took the proffered hand, Hayden Jones. I hope they treated you well, no roughing up? Agent Barrett was cordial, Hayden said. Did they tear the place up? Joseph asked, walking down the hallway peeking into doors. I'm not sure, Hayden said feeling a little defensive about not watching the agents better. No worries, said Joseph, you could not have stopped them if they had. How did you stop them, asked Hayden? I convinced the judge there was not a real solid amount of evidence when I went back over it with him and pointed out that Acacia has had no brushes with the law, and is an outstanding member of the community. The judge said he would allow the warrant if new evidence came to light. I doubt there will be more new evidence because I doubt Acacia has done anything to warrant it, Hayden assured him. Let us hope you are right, when Acacia does get a hold of you please have him contact me if you will, Hayden asked. Sure I'll tell him when he calls me. Thank you then, I'll be about my business.

You have a room for the night, asked Hayden. I have not gotten one yet, but I am sure there will be one I can get. You could stay here for the night, I wouldn't mind the company. There is a couch in the other room or you could use some blankets on the floor. Joseph thought about this for a moment, I am tired, he said, maybe I should stay and get an early start tomorrow. Where would you sleep then? There are four couches here I will use one of them, Hayden said.

Chapter Twenty Three

Acacia, Alexander and Brock have just landed and want to talk to you. Tamara was excited, Alexander and Brock had told her they had good news. Acacia followed Tamara to the dinning area where they both were eating trying to build back their strength from the long flight. Acacia sat down across from them and waited for them to get through. Alexander spoke first. He is squeaky clean, he said speaking of agent Barrett, we went through his home, found bank records, phone records bills, some mail a few days old setting on his desk. He was married but his wife recently died, care to know where she died and under what circumstances? I assume it is pertinent or you would not be asking me that? Got it in one, said Brock. She died because of one of our actions against Pierce, we didn't know there had been a casualty, said Alexander. That's not good, said Acacia, we watched and were extra careful, there were never any reports of deaths in any of what we did. You are right, said Brock, but she was in an accident with an emergency vehicle going to one of the sites to put out one of the fires we started. Somehow Barrett has put it together, we think he may even know little about us and these intrusions into our home are for him to gather more information to figure the rest of it out. The poor man, said Tamara, I feel really bad about it but we didn't have a choice. Tamara could see the news bothered Acacia, she went over to him. We were as careful as we could be, Brock said to Acacia, it is not your fault. Not it isn't really, Acacia agreed, but I still hate it.

He looked at the two dragons, did you find any real evidence that he might have learned more about us? No, said Alexander, I really can't see how he came to the conclusion about his wife if someone hadn't told him. Find out all you can about him, there has to be some relationship between him and Pierce then. Find out who his wife worked for if she did work, maybe the connection is there. Maybe you should go talk to him, suggested Tamara, maybe he would tell you. Maybe, said Acacia, Brock call Joseph and see if he can find out if agent Barrett or someone above him are behind this. Acacia took Tamara's hands, I might just talk to him as you suggested unless he is not the one behind it all. If he is only following orders from someone else it wouldn't do any good to ask him about it. Tamara kissed him softly, no worrying please, she said, it will all work out.

It's nine, said Tamara, you ready for bed? Sure, Acacia said, it's been a long day, I could use some sleep. Alexander and Brock had left so, Tamara slipped into the shower and turned on the water. She then went to Acacia and slipped his clothes off and lead him into the warm downpour that awaited them.

Acacia had called a meeting and all of the dragons were gathered around in the conference room at the resort. After they all had settled in and the waiter had delivered the drinks and each had ordered he called for their attention. First we go home tomorrow. There was not the response that Acacia had expected, it seemed that the dragons had enjoyed this vacation. Next, Acacia said, it seems that agent Barrett has been the one behind the investigations. He has been able to get his bosses to go along because of some photos of us carrying boxes when we did that job for Kincaid Monroe. It appears that Monroe was bringing some weapons illegally into the country and we had at his request carried some boxes from the plane to a waiting truck. This was being observed by the FBI and Barrett has taken it up as a personal vendetta because he has some way linked the death of his wife to us. She unfortunately was killed, hit by an emergency vehicle as they were on their way to one of the fires we set at one of their building to get them off our back. Acacia held up his hand, stalling any interruption, we do not know how he found out we were involved in the fires, but we know that his wife worked for Pierce. I believe the threat is from agent Barrett, I am going to talk to him, I will keep all of you updated, that is all I know for now.

Acacia and Tamara met out at a car they had hired, they were going to drive to see agent Barrett. Joseph had told Acacia that he was confident that the meeting wouldn't result in Acacias arrest. I would be a three hour drive and they had had Joseph arrange a meeting for them. They settled down for the drive and talked about their life and the children and the future of the dragons. Arriving only thirty minuets before the meeting they grabbed a quick lunch then drove to the meeting at the FBI building. They walked up to the information desk and Barrett was summoned to get them, he arrived and cordially escorted them to his office.

What can I do for you he asked across the desk after he had seated them and then himself. We believe there has been a mix up about us, said Acacia. We understand you have some evidence that you believe links us to a crime. We believe you were interested in obtaining more information about it, and about us to, to help you decide your actions about it. We would like to talk to you and get the matter cleared up. Thank you for coming in, Barrett responded, but I believe you have been helping a man to smuggle guns into the country. I intend to continue to investigate this until I am very confident you are not involved or until I have enough evidence to arrest you. But believe me I will follow up on this no matter what you do to try to dissuade me from it, is that clear Mr. Stone? Very clear, Acacia said, but coming and talking to you will help to show you we are interested in getting this settled as well, correct? Acacia waited for his response. Maybe, Barrett conceded, but if you are lying or try to hide anything from me I will know and I will do what ever it takes to get the truth. Fair, said Acacia, do you have any questions we can answer?

Yes there is, I have evidence that puts you at an offloading of illegal guns, we have pictures of you and some of your employees moving containers full of guns along with witnesses to testify you were there and participated. Then why haven't you arrested me and my men? I haven't gotten enough evidence to show you knew it was guns you were working with, but I will. No you won't, said Acacia, because we were there on a security job and were asked to help his men move the crates, we are innocent and you know it. What really is your issue, and how much longer do you think your bosses will keep going along with you? I have no issue but the enforcing of the law, Barrett said looking peeved. Well you will not be able to make this stick as I have signed documents showing that my team was there as security detail because of death threats made to my client, that is the only reason we were there and all of my men will testify so in any court you want to bring this to. My lawyer will be sending over signed affidavits to that effect later. Now any more problems from you and we will file a complaint of harassment with the FBI and follow it up as we have to. Now if this is all because of a more personal issue you have with us let me hear it now and we can settle that as well. It was apparent the agent Barrett was seething as he spoke, you are guilty and I will bring the full force of the FBI down to prove it, you are not above the law Mr. Stone. No, Acacia answered, anger evident in his voice, but neither are you.

Acacia stood, now are we free to leave? You may go, Barrett said through clenched teeth, but do not attempt to leave the state as you may be called in to be interviewed again. That is satisfactory, agreed Acacia, as kindly as he could muster.

In the car Tamara put her hand and on Acacia's leg, you are in the right, don't let him get to you. Let's call Joseph and tell him what happened and let the legal system deal with it. Yea, Acacia said putting his hand on hers, that is what I came up with also, we need to get this behind us so we can get on with the things we need to do in our lives. We have a job next week that will require all of our attention, I need to focused on that. Well let's get ourselves home and get focused, Tamara said seeing Acacia relax a bit, I'll call Joseph now and tell him what happened. Ok, Acacia said, he seemed happy for her to take the initiative.

The call to Joseph went well as he informed them that he was confident he could get agent Barrett off their backs, he also said he would get the papers ready, he needed them to sign so he could get them to get to the FBI by the end of the day. He also wanted to meet with them about some other matters and set up an appointment for the next day. The trip back to the compound went well and the children all came out to meet them as they drove in. They all called Acacia "cacia" now because Annabelle did and no matter what was said to them they wouldn't change. They were all eight years old and the dragons were so proud of all of them. Even though they were all of different personalities, they all were growing up and showing no signs of any major medical problems and they all were doing very well in their school work with most of them into sixth grade work.

The dragons would be starting to go around the compound naked more often as the children were soon to reach puberty and they were being left undressed more often then not. Even now many of the dragons were going about unclothed when indoors, Tamara found it disconcerting even though she knew the reason but she had made up her mind to do as they did. Therefore it did not surprise her when Acacia went inside and undressed and showered and left their apartment undressed to go to the ops. With in a week she and Susan were the only two except for

Hayden going about dressed, Hayden was very careful that no one saw him naked. Susan came up to her, if you had told me I would ever live in a house with a bunch of hot naked men a few years ago I would have called you nuts. Well, said Tamara, I feel I need to participate in this so I will be starting tomorrow. Acacia said I didn't have to, but they have found it helps the children to be naked if they aren't the only ones. Well it obviously doesn't bother them so why should it bother us, Susan said. Exactly, agreed Tamara, and with that they both slipped out of their clothes.

The only time any one was dressed was when they were going to leave for a job. So when Tamara found Acacia dressed the next morning she knew he was to be leaving soon. I thought you were going tomorrow, she said. We were supposed to but the client just called and they had to move their schedule up to today I just received the call so we are just now getting ready. Just then Annabelle came running into the room, seeing her father clothed she knew he was leaving and her face dropped. I know honey, he said before she could voice what he was sure had just ran through her mind, we were supposed to go riding tonight. Tamara had forgotten, but the dragons were going to take all the children for a ride on their backs tonight. Something they did to get them used to heights and flying. We will go when we get back he said, the client moved the schedule up on us. Ok, she said and hugged her fathers waist, Tamara had never seen a father and daughter as close as these two seem to be, but Annabelle was close to her as well. I'll miss you, Annabelle said to her father, you be safe, she added, something Tamara said every time that Acacia left and Annabelle had picked up on it. Ok dear, Acacia answered, the same he said to Tamara when she told him to be safe. Annabelle loved it and happily skipped out of the room. She's just like you, you know, Acacia said as her kissed he on the cheek. Loved by two wonderful women, how lucky can a man be.

Chapter Twenty Four

Leslie was in the library, he often took this time when they all were going about undressed to look for medical problems on all the people in his care. It was easier then the formal checkup in the office and his charges were being their selves and unguarded in their behavior. One thing that did happen in the dragon population was scoliosis in the dragons. He had provided therapy for two of the younger dragons when they had joined with Acacia, and two of the young dragons had needed the same in this new group. Though the dragon gene gave the dragons a curative power over the most common of diseases and illnesses, it didn't stop them from having deformities. He had not caught any thing upon initial check ups and the follow ups but that didn't mean there was not something new so he watched. This was the reason he was the one to see what happened. Devon the son of Roman was running after Perry who is William's son when his figure blurred. It was a odd thing, the outline of the person seemed to lose it's definition. Leslie went to get Roman so he could be the first to see his son change. Roman with him, they ran to where the boys were playing and stopped to watch them. The change often times occurred the first time for a dragon when they were focused and their mind was trying to perform a task, Leslie told Tamara as they watched, the dragon is not paying attention to anything else. As they watched he blurred again. This is early, said Leslie, but not unheard of. Already many of the dragons were gathered around watching as the news spread throughout the compound. Devon was trying to catch Perry, who obviously was faster, he wanted to get something he was keeping from him. Perry was staying out of his grasp, as he was taunting him, waving his hand over his head. After catching his breath for a moment Devon started running after him again with the sun sparkling off their bodies catching the dragon skin as they ran about the garden. Suddenly to everyone's surprise Devon changed into a deep blue dragon, his wings spread and he was lifted off his feet for a short moment before he changed back again. There were cheers all around and they all gathered to clap Roman on the back and congratulate him. Devon finally caught Perry and oblivious to the excitement they went off to play together. Tamara watched them as they passed through a door into the house surprised that Devon thought that changing into his dragon form was no big deal, maybe, she thought, he didn't even know he had turned into a dragon.

The worse day ever since being with the dragons occurred only a few days later. Acacia and Tamara were in the den when shouting broke out in the formal living room and the sound of fighting. Then they heard a cry of pain as they were rushing to see what the problem was. To their shock they entered the room to find Agent Barrett with a knife attempting to cut Roman with it. Tamara looked around to see Leslie with a long gash from just over his pubic area to between his breast with the blood dripping off his penis in a steady stream. She turned just in time to see agent Barrett in an unbelievable fast rush cut Roman in the side of the neck and the blood poured out as Roman slapped his hand over the cut. Then in complete shock she watched as Acacia jumped an impossible height into the air and changed, with a smooth and preternatural speed reached out with his claw and grabbed the agents head and twisted. There was a dull snap and the agent fell to the floor.

Tamara reached Leslie who was watching Roman, get us both to the infirmary if he is to live he said between teeth clenched from the pain. And quickly get some additional pressure on his wound. Also get me Brock, and hurry. Susan supporting a badly cut Ben came into the room. Ben had been cut in the inner thigh as the agent had tried to sever the artery there, a tee shirt was tied around his thigh. Tamara and Acacia rushed Leslie and Roman to the infirmary as Susan ran to find Brock. Anyone else hurt, Acacia asked Ben. Albert, said Ben, he seems to be unconscious but alright. Have someone bring him down to the infirmary Acacia said over his shoulder to Ben. In the infirmary Tamara watched as Acacia taking the disinfectant began to clean the blood from Leslie from his breast down. As he did Leslie taped the wound back shut. Acacia tenderly cleaned the last of the blood off him and to Tamara's shock Leslie closed his eyes and seemed to go to sleep. Forest, who was holding pressure on Romans neck shouted, were loosing him, fear evident in his voice, he is passing out. Tamara turned to Acacia who's attention was fully on Leslie. She was expecting him to go to Roman. But Acacia was focused on Leslie. Tamara watched as the wound on Leslie's body began to heal at an unbelievable rate. When it was sealed but not completely healed Leslie crumpled into Acacia's waiting arms. Acacia laid him back and began to administer mouth to mouth and soon Leslie moved and woke.

Acacia handed him a candy bar and helped him over to Roman. Brock walked in the room and seeing what was happening immediately laid down on the table that was next to the one Roman was on. Leslie with unbelievable speed started a transfusion and began to work on the cut at Roman's neck. It was just a few minuets and the bleeding was stopped and Leslie relaxed and slowed his movements. A few minuets later Roman's eyes opened and he looked around. Welcome back, Acacia said. Roman smiled I made it. Leslie smiled down at him, try to sleep, you will heal faster if you do, I'll wake you to eat in about an hour, you should be able to then. With a peaceful expression Roman was asleep in seconds. Ben hobbled in supported by Susan. Acacia handed Leslie another candy bar and he ate while he worked. After a few moments later Albert was carried into the room. Is he the last one? Asked Acacia to William and Peter who had carried him in. Yes, said William. Leslie checked out Albert, he will be fine after a little, no concussion, but he will have a major headache. Give him these he said pouring some pills out of a bottle and then keep him awake for at least twenty four hours. With that Leslie slipped into a bed there in the infirmary and was immediately asleep.

What happened, Acacia asked William. It looks as though the agent rang to enter the gate and Albert recognizing him let him in. I believe he was on his way to get us when he was accosted by the agent. He knew he was FBI and so was not suspecting. The agent attacked everyone he came into contact with after that, he didn't realize how thick dragon skin is and how hard to cut or we would have had some casualties. We almost lost Roman as it was, said Acacia, if Leslie had been hurt worse we never would have made it in time to help him. The question now is what to do about agent Barrett, his death will bring scrutiny on us, William said. Alexander who had been listening said, what did he arrive in? Looks like his personal car, answered William. Leave it to me then said Alexander, I'll put him in it and drive it off the steep cliff down the hill. How are you going to do that? There will have to be skid marks and signs of an attempt to stop. I'll drive it off, jump and change as it falls, said Alexander. You will never make it, said William, concern in his voice. I'll make it, said Alexander,

I've done things like it before. You sure? Asked Acacia, we could probably find another way. You have to agree this would be best, asked Alexander. Well yes, agreed William but not worth losing you. I'll make it no problem, Alexander looked at Acacia for approval. Acacia nodded his head in approval, go ahead he said.

Next thing is how was he able to move so fast, he can not be completely human, said William. I know, agreed Acacia, get a swab from his mouth before Alexander takes him, an autopsy would be better but we can't cut him up and it look like an accident. You need to find out everything you can on the man, I'm worried there are more like him and we are in danger from them. That is my worry as well, said William, I'm going to post guards for a while until we get more information, no one gets in or out unless you or me know and approves it. Good said Acacia, keep me informed. Tamara followed him out of the room. He started talking as they left not giving her time for the question so heavy on her mind. It is an ability we have but it kills us. If no one is there to revive you, you die. Sometimes you die anyway, Leslie risked his life for Roman's a very brave thing to do. You knew he was going to do it before he did though? Tamara asked. I suspected.

Tamara watched as the sinews of his body move in time to his movements, her thoughts turned to the erotic, how strange the thoughts that a close call with danger makes a person think of. Acacia must have sensed her thoughts as he pulled her into a storage shed and made love to her in hard thrusts and deep passion. They went to their room to shower. William knocked on the door and entered as they both stepped from the shower. Alexander is ready and the swab is with Leslie, do you want to go? Yes, Acacia said as he began to dress, be there shortly.

Alexander slipped the seats of the black car back to it's farthest position. They posted dragons to watch for cars coming but so far no one had driven by. They placed agent Barrett in the drivers seat and Alexander sat in his lap. He check to be sure he could exit the car easily and then he started it and drove toward the cliff.

He hit the dirt on the side of the road and with expert precision spun the car in a circle in the dirt and then drove straight off the cliff. Acacia held his breath as they waited for him to appear above the cliff so they would know he had made it clear. They heard the crash of the car on the rocks and after what seemed far to long, Alexander in dragon form flew up over the cliff edge and changed and landed before them. Let's get out of here, he said.

The next few days were intense, after a spot in the local paper about the crash, they all waited to see if the agent's death would strike up a investigation and if the investigation would turn toward them. But as the days passed their was no phone calls about it, nor any inquires. They settled back into their routine and their lives filled with work and the children. All of the children could now assume dragon form, it seemed that Devon's change set off a cascade, soon they were all starting to change.

The dragons threw a big party after the last child had changed and invited almost everyone they had dealings with. Acacia was standing in a corner watching the different guest Tamara standing beside him. She was admiring him in his tuxedo he was still looking like a twenty four year old and she had now caught up to him in age according to their looks, they were a very good looking pair she thought. Joseph his lawyer and long time friend stepped up beside him. Some day you will have to tell me why you do not seem to age, he said, taking Tamara's hand and kissing it as he had seen the dragons do. I have a feeling you already know, answered Acacia. Joseph chuckled, maybe I do. There is talk of an investigation into your business, it is just talk now but I will keep you informed. Thanks Joseph , Acacia said, and thanks for coming to the party. My pleasure, it is a nice break from the rat race.

Where is Mara? Asked Acacia, asking about his wife. She is on one of her crusades, he answered, you are lucky to have found a wife with the same interest as yourself. He nodded toward Tamara as he spoke. She does do a plenty of good deeds for us both, helps my reputation. I have noticed your business has been busy lately, that is good in this current economy, Joseph said. We are going international, said Acacia, we need more work for the new employees. You are keeping them busy, asked Joseph. Yes, we are now, it was a little slow for a few months, but now we have more work then we can do and are turning it down. Good, said Joseph, because I'm a little worried about this investigation. It seems to be coming from up higher then the last. I'll keep you informed but you be ready for anything. Joseph shook hands with Acacia, it's been good. As he walked away into the crowd,

Acacia looked a Tamara, he is worried. So am I, said Tamara. Tamara was looking a Leslie who was obviously intrigued by a woman at the bar. He was making the woman laugh and when she did Leslie would move closer to her. Voluptuous was an understatement for the woman, she was close to three hundred pounds. Acacia followed her gaze and watched as well. The woman was laughing again and Leslie placed his hand on her side just below her breasts. She in return placed her hand on the inside of his thigh and rubbed, occasionally hitting the bulge of his pants. Leslie leaned in and whispered something in her ear and she responded with a nod of agreement. She then stood and slowly worked her way into the hall adjacent to the bar and in a moment Leslie followed her. Tamara smiled, he likes the large women, she said to Acacia. He shrugged, I never knew if he did, no one has said anything about it before.

Tamara's focus turned to Annabelle who was talking to Brock on a sofa in a nook set a little aside from the room. They were both in deep conversation, Brock was intently listening to what ever she was saying. In another corner of the room Roman and Forest were intently talking to a man Tamara recognized as one of their suppliers. The actions of the man told her they were not talking work, but they were all very interested in what ever they were talking about. It was then she saw William with an older woman sitting in a corner. He was taking telling a story with his hands waving and making gestures the woman occasionally placing her hand on his knee. William looked almost thirty, the woman a late fifty, she was obviously enjoying the attention of what she thought was a younger man. Tamara was intrigued, William had never shown any interest in a woman before. Tamara shook Acacia's sleeve to get his attention. She gestured to William and smiled. Acacia took in the scene for a moment and said, now that is worth the whole party. Tamara hugged his arm, yes what ever it cost that is worth every penny. Tamara turned to look at William and the woman again but they were gone.

It was Sunday and Tamara awoke to Acacia nibbling her nipple, when she awoke, he rolled on top of her and deliciously slid in. They showered and he asked her what she wanted to do today. Relax with you, you can tell me all that is going on and we can catch up. Ok, but breakfast first, he countered, I suppose we can wait until after we eat. They were sitting out side under a small tree that they had had the landscaper plant and ring it with a bench. The children were here and there playing and talking, some with their parents and some with their father, it was a good scene, it left a warm feeling in Tamara's heart to be part of this all. It was an unusual family, but it was her family. She loved them all and would do anything to protect them and see them happy. Brock and Annabelle stepped out of a doorway, they were again deep in conversation. Tamara nudged Acacia and pointed at them, can you find out what they talk about so much? I'll ask, he said, William may know, but she is growing up and you can not hold her down. Your right, she agreed, forget it. No, I'll ask, there is something they have in common, I would like to know also. Speaking of William do you know how he came out? He was smiling this morning, he doesn't do that often. Good she laughed, I never thought I would see him interested in a lady like he was last night. He likes the ladies but his work takes precedent, that's all, Acacia said. He was hurt quite bad once by a woman, I never got all of the story from him but he never seemed to get over it. Well he scored last night and I'm happy he did, Tamara said.

Monday came and the dragons all left for various jobs and left Tamara to monitor the com and Susan began to get emergency items to gather for a quick exit. They had taken Joseph's warning to heart, and Tamara, Acacia, Ben, Susan and William had put together a list of items to gather to one place. The items were bagged in bags a dragon could carry in his claws and each one weighed close to the same and not so heavy as to burden the flyer. Clothes food and essentials, data disk and all that would be needed to move and continue to work. They were not sure yet where to go, as that was still in decision. Susan between putting the items together was also monitoring the children's studies. They had found a video system that taught the children, all of them being in the same grade helped a lot. They watched the videos and then did the work. They were tested once a week. The children were testing high and had a good deal of leisure time as well. The system was working perfectly. They were at the age to be in fifth grade but were testing into the tenth grade, soon they would be eligible for college work soon. Tamara left the com for a break and to see if all was going well with Susan when the door bell rang.

There was a car at the gate and it looked like the woman William had been with was driving alone. Tamara signaled the gate to open and went out to meet the woman as she drove up the drive. She stepped out of her car and Tamara realized she was a knockout for her age. I would like to speak to William, she said as she walked up and shook hands with Tamara. He is not here at the moment, Tamara said, but you are welcome to come in. The woman hesitated, he said he worked here. He does Tamara agreed, he is currently on the jobsite and will not be back for two days, is there a way I can help you. The woman gave Tamara an appraising look, I'm not sure, she said. I just wanted to speak with him. He will be back late Wednesday, if you don't want to come in I will tell him you came by. Again the woman visibly hesitated, she seemed to be caught in-between two thoughts. Finally she said it seemed strange he worked here and also lived here. Tamara understood what the problem was, he is a good friend of my husbands, they have worked together for years, he has no attachments and so lives here with some of the other employees as we have plenty of room. The woman became relieved when Tamara said he was not attached. Tamara decided to tell her more. He has not been attached for as long as I have known him about eleven years, he is a really kind and responsible man. The woman smiled at that, he is kind she said. Come in and we can talk more, Tamara gestured into the open door. He is kind, she said again, as she stepped toward the door. Susan was just inside having heard the bell and Tamara introduced them. Susan smiled conspiratorially at Tamara when she realized who the woman was. So happy to meet you, Susan said, adding, William talks constantly about you. He does, said the woman, he is kind, she said again to no one in particular.

Do you want to talk to him a moment? Asked Tamara. Oh yes, she said quickly, it would be all right with him at work? Well I have to get back to the com anyway, I monitor the radio traffic for my husband, we should be able to talk to him for a moment. That would be good, she said excited. The woman had fallen for William all the way, Tamara could tell, but how would she take finding out he was older then her and a dragon? Time would have to tell that. Tamar took her to ops and they both sat down together. Tamara listen to the talk and found a place to let William and the other dragons know they were being listened to by an outsider. Lisa! William said with true excitement when he knew it was her. Lisa actually tittered in excitement herself. I didn't know you were coming by, I thought I had explained I would be away for a few days. Oh, you did, she said I just wanted to see you and thought you might not have left yet. I do want to see you, William said, but we left this morning early. You have my number then, she asked. Yes, William said, I have it I programmed it into my phone, I'll call you on my way back, you will be able to take the call, he asked. Yes, I'll be waiting. Ok, my dear, see you then, William said. Tamara smiled, they were both smitten, and now she knew she was not just a fling. Thank you so much, the woman took her hand, I will be going now. I'll show you out, Tamara said.

They talked girl talk as they walked to the entrance. It is a little strange but I understand him living here with you and your husband. Tamara took the opportunity to get her ready for the truth, we actually have quite a few of our employees living on the grounds, it's part of the employment package they can take advantage of if they like. I'm sure it is good for some she said. She waved good bye and drove out. Well, thought Tamara, we'll see wont we.

The dragons were only just back when Lisa rang at the gate, William let her in and went out to meet her. Tamara had told him she had come by to investigate if he had been truthful with her, so William had been very careful to let her know he was very interested. She was coming over for him to take her out to dinner, but the idea was also for her to meet all the dragons and get a feel for how many people lived at the estate. William was going to try to judge her reaction also when he revealed he was a dragon, she was older and would not take to the unusual and any change very well. Susan brought her into the formal living room and little by little the dragons came in to meet her. Tamara could tell she was uncomfortable with the amount of people living together, no doubt to her it reminded her of the communes that had sprouted up in her earlier years. After introducing her to all of the dragons

William sat beside her and made small talk but talk that told her of the life they had all here to gather. He was trying to make her see they were just good friends and live together out of convenience. We each have our own place, her told her, would you care to see my bungalow? She reddened a little but said yes. William took her out to walk across the courtyard to his place, I really am happy you came to see me. I know you are not really comfortable with us all living together here but we really do it out of convenience, there are no weird things going on between us. I really didn't think there was she said, but I always lived with my husband and the children, I'm a bit old fashioned. I know and I like that in you, but there is something I need to show you, and out of respect I want to show you now before we get farther involved. Lisa stiffened, you are married then? No, William laughed, nothing like that. William took her hands in his, It's just I am different in a way that you need to know and if I lose you over it, it is better then deceiving you. Lisa visibly relaxed, we're all different in some way.

Well I am human but with a twist. Lisa just looked at him. I need to get naked to show you is that all right. I have seen naked men before, she said blushing deeply. William stopped outside of his quarters, you may be afraid but you are safe with me, you understand? She nodded her understanding. William watched her as he undressed, she looked around to see if anyone was watching him but all of the dragons were inside with Acacia and were watching from there. When William was down to only his shorts he asked her if she was ok. You are going to show me now, she asked. Well I have to take these off, he said, motioning to his shorts. Not out here, she whispered. I have to show you out here, he said. She looked around and not seeing anyone else, she then shrugged. William watched her turn bright red as he dropped his shorts. Turning he asked her if she could see the sparkle of his skin. Yes, she answered stepping forward as if to touch him then remembered herself. You can touch me if you want. It's beautiful, she said, is this what you wanted to show me? No, said William, step back and I will change into a dragon, but do not scream, promise? She laughed a nervous laugh, really William, this is making me very uncomfortable. William changed, Lisa screamed and fell back sitting hard on the ground.

William changed back and ran over to her. Lisa jerked away from him, how did you do that William, that is not funny. She tensed as he sat beside her crossing his legs, I am a dragon, all of us except Tamara and Susan are, we live together for protection. She was flushing at his nakedness so close. You want me to put my clothes back on he asked. No! she said abruptly, no she corrected. She reached out and touched his skin at his shoulder, it is rougher, her hand slid down onto his chest, it is beautiful. My intentions are to marry you and make you happy, he said taking her hand in his, but I had to show you first you understand that now don't you? She gestured minutely to his genitals, everything works? He laughed, yes very well. Can we have children, I don't want children, but if you…she stopped. Would you be a dragon again? Can you be anytime you want?

I can one more time now for you, he said. He got up and backing a little away he changed. Folding his wings so he looked as little as he could he bent down and kissed her cheek. A tear was in her eye, she reached slowly and touched his jaw. I've fallen in love with you, she said, after ten years and not wanting anyone else, I've fallen in love with you. William changed and fell to the ground beside her. I have also, said William, it seemed I would never get over this one bad experience but I am. Lisa rubbed his chest smoothing down the hairs, what will my children say? I hope they will be happy, William said, when can I meet them? They will be visiting in a few weeks, then would be good I suppose.

William rolled on his side where he was facing his bungalow. William she laughed, your hard. He chuckled, I would take you inside and make love to you but I am not sure if that is the proper way to treat you. It would be proper, she said. Tamara watched as William and Lisa walked into his quarters holding hands and knew all was going to be alright. She thought of Timothy, he had shown the girl that drove the delivery truck that he was a dragon, they had dated a while but then no more. They had to threaten her to keep her silent. William and Acacia had flown to her apartment and explained to her that if she told anyone they would come back and no one could stop them. I looked as if she had remained silent. They had known not everyone would be open to the idea they were dragons but so far they had come out good.

Tamara went out to meet the dragons after they had been away for almost a week on a very complicated job. Most of them were driving in but William and Brock were flying in and would land any moment. A very happy Lisa was standing beside of Tamara waiting for her lover to show up. She had refused to marry William but had asked to move some of her things in with him and she now was there with him more then at her house. William was making her happier then anyone Tamar had ever seen. Tamara had found her to be incredibly smart if a little backward. The woman had her own opinions but rarely expressed them in words but they were obvious in her actions. She never was seen naked, always when you saw her she was fixed up and was proper, polite, and had William always in her protection, you dared not say anything negative about William. She didn't seem to mind her lover parading around naked as the dragons did often, and when the other dragons were naked she politely kept her eyes up on their faces. With William at her side she was all laughter, smiles and giggles and teasing. She adored him, and Tamara thought that she liked to see him naked amongst the others as he was very endowed and she liked to show him off. William obliged her every whim.

His performance at work was off the charts, a hard thing to accomplish as he was already very adept at his job. When Tamara would mention them, Acacia would just chuckle and say, "he is happy". William changed and landed so close to Lisa that he was able to embrace her without moving forward. She jumped at his performance and passionately kissed him. Tamar could see that the flyers were very weary and offer them food and drink, William just grabbed two items with a heartfelt thanks, and grabbed Lisa by the hand and they were off to his quarters. Lisa knew very little about him and when he would try to tell her she shushed him saying, "I like you exotic." Acacia came up to her and hugged her with a hug that told her he was so glad to see her. Maybe we should follow their lead, he said, motioning toward William and Lisa. We should, said Tamara. Annabelle came out to see her father, she hugged him and kissed him on the cheek. Welcome home dad. Thanks sweet heart. Go rest, she said, I'll see you later. I'll do that baby, thanks.

He and Tamara went to their room. They stripped and stepped into the shower. Tamara gave him a massage and he returned the favor. It will be nine soon, you want to go straight to bed? She asked him. I'm not sleepy yet, maybe in an hour. She toweled him off as he stretched. He did the same for her. The door bell rang and a few minuets Alexander came on the intercom to say there was a delivery for him. Bring it up if you don't mind Acacia asked. Alexander came in the door and handed Acacia the envelope. When Acacia opened it he called Alexander back into the room. Call a meeting immediately in the ops. What is it? Tamara asked. Trouble, Joseph says to get out of the country as fast as we can, take only what we need. We are not to use our phones. Tell everyone. Where's Annabelle, Tamara asked him. I don't know, but as you look for her tell everyone no phone calls. Look in the library, she is with Brock there sometimes, or at the pool. Tamara told Peter, and Alexander no phones and about the meeting as she passed them on the way to the library. She told Albert, Ben, and Susan, on her way to the pool. She saw Annabelle and Brock out side as she passed a window and went out to see them. She told them what she knew and they left to go to ops. She stopped at William's door and knocked. He came to the door, get clothes on and meet us all at ops in ten minuets, we are leaving as soon as we can.

They all waited until William and Lisa showed up and then all of them were there. Acacia began, Joseph called, he said we are in danger, he is not sure what will happen but the news from a friend in the FBI is that they will raid very soon maybe tonight. Joseph has never been wrong before so gather your things for a few days, only what you can get into a bag. There are pre-prepared bags in the storage if you prefer, your name will be on them. He turned to the children. We will be flying, all of us. This will be your first true flight from home, stay by your fathers side, let him know if you tire. He turned toward Lisa, you have to make a decision. We have done nothing to call this down upon us except to protect ourselves from being killed. If you go with us you will have to ride on William's back in flight. You are free to go back home and wait until we sort this out and William can come to you. She turned to William, I go where he does. William hugged her.

There is a group of hotels on the beach here, William pointed to a satellite map, we will each in a group of five check in to one of them, cash only. Land here behind these trees and change, get dressed and wait for your group leader, you have been told who they are. Stay close and watch out for each other. They each filed out to the garden. The last of the lights were turned out in the houses. All the door were locked. The dragons all changed, Tamara helped Lisa onto William and then climbed on to Acacia. Tamara heard Lisa let out a little scream as the dragon jumped into the air and they were off. Tamara kept a close eye on Annabelle and all the other children but they were having a time of it. Phillip the son of Albert was doing small dives and flips as he flew. Drew was also showing off making circles around Timothy his father. The rest including Annabelle were weaving as they went. Tamara bent down to kiss Acacia on the neck and he returned the gesture and his big head came around to nibble her ear. The trip seemed short to Tamara as in a few minuets it seemed they were landing. They grouped up and went to find a room. William and Lisa went with Annabelle, Acacia, and Tamara. Four of the boys grouped up with Brock, they all liked to be with Brock. Susan, Ben and Cameron took two of the other boys and the others grouped together. William will come and find you all, we will get room numbers so we can talk. They all went their separate ways.

Acacia took out the radios they used to reach the hybrid dragons and tried again to reach them. It is to late for anyone to be monitoring the radios he said, it will take to long for Alexander to fly to them and he would be to tired to fly tonight if he did. I need to drive to Joseph's house to tell him how to get a hold of us, you want to go? He asked Tamara. Yes she said after you shower you smell. I'll shower you go tell William and Lisa we will be going. When Tamara explained to William that they hadn't been able to reach the hybrids by radio, Lisa overhead them say it was in orange county. She inquired where and upon hearing where she told them a friend lived a short ways away and he would not mind her calling him and asking him to go tell them. You see, she explained, he stays up late playing poker with his army friends, he will drop by if I ask. Ask him to go by please, and let me know what happens, said Tamara before returning to her room. Before they left for Josephs they told Annie to mind the radio as they were expecting a response from the other dragons and give them the number to the hotel, they would call her from the road. Annabelle was very excited with the cloak and dagger going on and took a pad from the bedside and wrote all they said down.

Acacia opened the door of the cab for her and she slid in. The cab was a new one and the usual smells didn't assault her nose. Acacia gave the driver an address a block from Josephs and they sat back and relaxed. It was twenty minuets before they stopped in front of a house in a very nice neighborhood. They got out and waited until the cab was out of view, Acacia slipped behind a bush and changed. Tamar picked up his clothes and he took her by the shoulders he took flight. They circled Joseph's house three times before they were comfortable to land on the second floor balcony at the back. Joseph came to the door and slid back the curtain, he was naked and when he saw them there he quickly closed the curtain. They heard another male voice, Acacia and Tamara looked at each other, and then the curtain slid back again.

Joseph was there in his robe and opened the door. I've had a raccoon on the balcony before and thought it was him again, sorry about that. No we're sorry, we had no way of letting you know we were coming. Tamara noticed the bed was fully uncovered and was sure that he had had a lover with him. We hope we didn't come at a time to cause you a big problem but we needed to bring you this phone we picked up on the way over, it's a throw away one. She handed him the phone she had in her hand. Joseph looked out onto the balcony and said, you will need to explain how you got onto my balcony some day you know. Don't let it worry you there are no one around who can do the same. Call us early if you can and thanks for the warning. What is it you have done to bring this action down on you, asked Joseph. I will explain tomorrow, but just know we didn't do anything truly wrong, someone is after us and I will find out who. See you in the morning then, I'll show you out. Your friend he will not say anything? Acacia asked. No, he is my assistant bound by the same rules as me, lawyer client and all that. Where are you going Acacia? Not sure yet, Mexico is the closest. I have a friend with some bungalows he rents in Mexico, I've been there they are nice, I'll call him tomorrow and see if they are available. That sounds great Joseph, where in Mexico? Just past the border. Yea, call him, and good night then and thanks. Good night Acacia, and good luck.

Fly me back, Tamara said to Acacia, it's summer, we can land on the top of the hotel, I want to ride you nude. Acacia chuckled, we haven't done that for a while, ok, sure, why not. Tamara and Acacia stripped and she gather their clothes and he changed. In the room behind them Joseph almost jumped out of his skin, so that was their secret. A real dragon, he had thought maybe vampires really did exist after all the movies and TV shows. He decided then and there that where ever the dragons went he would go to, they after all would be in the middle of history, and he would be also, someday he would be known as the lawyer of the dragons, no one would forget Joseph Milliner. Tamara felt the same thrill as the first time she had rode on Acacia's back as he launched himself into the night sky, it was erotic ridding there naked the wind rustling the hairs on your whole body and tickling the places where no one but Acacia ever touched. Why did she have to grow old, she wished to be with Acacia and the dragons forever. They made her feel alive, invincible, strong, wild, she felt the part of the dragon queen. Acacia's head came around and he gently nibbled her nipple, he loved nipples, he was on hers constantly when they were together, often in public he would brush her as if on accident. Tamara scratched behind the tiny dragon ears, he loved to be scratched there when in dragon form, she was on fire and decided to treat him to something else when they landed. She pulled his head to her and whispered into his ear, don't change when you land I want in your flap for a while.

All was going well for the dragons. They now had communications to everyone they needed and Joseph had gotten them some small cottages in Mexico. They had arraigned for the hybrids to meet them there and they all were flying out today to go there themselves. Acacia had all their cash in an account in Mexico and they were going to be all right. The flight to Mexico was uneventful though a little long. They followed the map Tamara had and flew high enough that the road and highways matched what the map showed. They finally landed in a courtyard in the dead of night. There was twenty cottages. Two were occupied until late tomorrow. The hybrids came out to greet them and they divide up the rooms that were left. It would be crowded until they found some other place for the hybrids, maybe the resort behind them. The dragons were eating the candy bars that Susan was handing out, Tamara also handed out water in bottles. A shipment of supplies would be arriving tomorrow, the hybrids would unpack as the dragons slept late. Tamar went to the cottage that was theirs and started to unpack the small bag she had with her, there was an extra two beds squeezed into the room. Annabelle and three more boys were to share with them tonight. Tamara sighed, there was so much to do, sleep would be hard with so much on her mind. She was in the middle of changing into her night wear when Acacia came in. He hugged her and stripped and slipped into the bed. She slipped into bed beside him. He kissed her hard and long and then putting his arms around her hugged her again. He was asleep in seconds, she was also in only a few minuets.

Chapter Twenty Five

Three weeks later after coming back from a job, Brock was in his bedroom having showered and slipped into bed. He had just reached over and flipped the light off when he heard the door to his cottage open. He looked into the mirror that reflected on the door to see who it was, he wasn't expecting any one as they all had their own cottages now. He sat up when he realized it was Annabelle. Annie, what are you doing here? Hey Brock, she said, as she came around the end of a wall that blocked his view of the door. I came to talk to you. She dropped the robe she was wearing to the floor and stood naked before him. Annie, he exclaimed! What's gotten into you? She watched as he started to get up from the bed then realizing his erect condition he stopped. Annie, you know your father will kill us both if he finds out about you being here like this. She came over to him and sat on the bed beside him, her hand brushing his erection as she did. I arouse you, she asked quietly? Annie, I don't know what your thinking but you need to leave and we will discuss what ever you want tomorrow, I promise, ok? I want something from you Annie went on as if he hadn't spoken, and I want to ask it now. She stared into his eyes as she spoke. Annie this is very inappropriate. You are eleven, I am a grown man over one hundred years old, you must leave now. I won't mention a word of this to anyone if you just go now.

Annie reached over and stroked the hairs of his chest, I want you to mate with me in the next circle. No! Absolutely not! He all but shouted Oh, but you will. The way she said it made him stop short of his next words. Your father will never allow it Annie. On what grounds? She asked him slyly. He stopped short again. There had to be some reason, but for now he couldn't think of one. She went on, there has never been any rule that would restrict a person who wanted to and was able to perform the mating. I know, I checked them all. You have mated with women that were twenty and you were over a hundred then. But you are only eleven! He said, stress showing in his voice. My age is not really the issue is it? It is because I am the daughter of Acacia, is that not the truth. Partly he agreed. You see that is why I chose you, you have integrity, the most integrity of all the dragons. Some of the dragons would have already taken me up on my offer. I'm not so sure of that, he said. Her hand moved down to his lower abdomen. Annie, he warned holding her wrist stopping her. See, that is why I need you. Brock, I have chosen you, you will be my only mate. We will start a family together, we will live together for the rest of our time. Annie? Yes she responded looking deep into his eyes, Why now? Why not wait until next circle. At next circle I will be twenty three, I can not wait until then, the dragons must become strong, we must grow as fast as we can. With you with me, I can make them strong and be what my destiny requires of me.

Do you love me Brock, She asked? He could see it took a lot for her to ask that. He thought, not wanting her to be hurt by some stray word, he had to be careful. I will say yes Annie, her face lit up. He stopped her from saying anything more. Annie I must qualify it though. Go ahead I'm ready to hear what ever you say, she said her face becoming calm, say it straight, not beating around the bushes. Well, he said, then here it is. You know all the time we have spent together like brother and sister? She nodded affirmative. Ok, well, well I have felt attracted to you yes, but I never have let it enter my mind what you are asking. I didn't because it would betray Acacia and your mother. But give me time to examine my feelings, and time for you to grow up a little more, I believe it would be a solid yes. A smile came on her face. I would make you a good mate, she said, and you just need to get over that feeling that I am a child, you will soon know that I am no longer a child. But as for waiting, we can't. We have to wait, Brock assured her. No we can't, I am the one who has the power that my father was expecting to get. I've had it for about a week now, and I know what I want and I will get it one way or another. And one of the things I want is you in the circle. And after that I will build the dragons into an empire.

Annie, you must talk to your parents, Brock told her. No, you will tell them. Why me? You will tell them, she went on, exactly how I came to you, and how you told me to leave, that I would not go and that I want to mate in this circle. Why, he asked? One, they will take you serious, two, it will force their hand as they will not like me coming to you like this. Brock I am in love with you, I have been for a good amount of time. I know I'm young, I know I must seem very young to you. But I will be the next dragon leader, I need a good, intelligent, strong man beside me, but more especially a man with the integrity that you have deep in you. With power there is the terrible chance of misuse. I have a great power, I need someone I trust to keep me from misusing it. That someone is you, that is why it must be now. He smiled at her, give me sometime to get used to this and think about what you said. We will talk tomorrow and then I'll talk to your parents. She slipped off the bed and bending way to far over picked up her robe and slipped it on, tomorrow then. He watched her as she slipped out the door. Brock fell back on the bed, damn, he muttered. He looked down at his still erect member and shaking his finger at it, and you, you need to straighten up your act. His life living with all the dragons had been easy and smooth up until now, but now he had no idea what was to become of him, how would Acacia take this?